# JUST FAKE MARRIED

*Just... Book 1*

## MARTY VEE

Copyright © 2022 by Marty Vee

All rights reserved.

No portion of this book may be reproduced in any form without written permission from the publisher or author, except as permitted by U.S. copyright law.

# Newsletter Fun!

I love my newsletter, it's my favorite way to connect with my readers. Stay in the know about exciting news, upcoming releases, fun stuff, and freebies.  https://www.subscribepage.com/martyvee

# DEDICATION

*To all the best pups, we don't deserve you.*

# Contents

# Chapter 1

## Emmeline

I ran through the silvery bursts of my breath as my arms pumped at my sides in pace with my legs as my ponytail swung from side to side. Despite the freezing temperatures, sweat dampened my hairline. The path ran along the river. The ice reached from one bank to the other, but the flowing water hadn't frozen over yet. The city traffic was elevated at the top of the embankment.

To my left, Owen's feet landed in perfect stride with mine. His hazel eyes fixed to the middle distance, his face stern and lovely.

"What are you doing for Christmas?" I asked. We were more than halfway through our five-mile jog, and he'd been even quieter than usual.

"Family stuff. You?"

Another runner approached from the opposite direction, and Owen fell back behind me, before joining at my side again.

"Same. Spending Christmas Eve at Mom and Dad's—it's tradition. My brother Malcolm and his husband Tom do, too. So, we celebrate for about forty-eight hours. It's… a lot of family time." The cold air bit my lungs, but we kept an easy pace. "You going back home?"

I caught Owen's nod out of the corner of my eye. "Around Grand Rapids, right?"

He nodded again.

If I wanted a chatty running partner, I should have befriended someone else from the running group where I met him. Owen and I had gotten to know each other over the past eleven months, but this level of silence was a bit much, even for him. I'd told him about my work week and a TV show I had watched, a book I wanted to read, and the holiday shopping I still had to get done. It was all a shortened running version, but that was hardly the point. And all he'd said was hello and *"Family stuff. You?"*

I was due some reciprocal conversation.

"What's your deal?" I slowed my pace slightly. "You need to slow down?"

He glanced at me for the first time in about a mile before he focused back on the trail ahead. "No. Why?"

I meant to elbow him, but we weren't close enough. Instead, I passed through the air between us. "You've hardly spoken."

"Thinking."

"About...?"

His sculpted chest rose with an inhale.

We were almost the same height, though he was possibly an inch taller than me. In our many jogs together, I'd collected knowledge about his lean frame. He was attractive, if compactly built men were my type. I tended to go for tall and lean, but over the past few months, Owen had tipped the needle in his direction.

Owen was becoming my type.

Not tall or lean, not compactly built.

Just Owen.

I hadn't even realized my crush on him had gradually developed until I noticed how often I caught myself thinking about him and smiling—or how much I wondered what he looked like under his clothes. Unlike other men I knew, Owen always wore a shirt while working out, even on the hottest days—even if it clung to him like a second skin carving along the ridges of his chest, stomach, and arms.

Of course, currently, he wore layers under a slim-cut coat, unzipped to his waist to ward off the bitter cold.

"I have a donor's New Year's Eve party. I didn't go last year, and he mentioned it to my boss." A crease formed between Owen's eyebrows. Long black eyelashes lowered over his hazel eyes.

Even though Owen wasn't one to talk, I knew he was passionate about the dog rescue he worked for. As a veterinarian, he could probably make more money elsewhere and he wouldn't have to deal with donors, but he loved the dogs.

I wove around a frozen puddle. "Do you have to go?"

"Kinda."

"Is it really that big of a deal? It's just an appearance, right?"

"I hate these things. The donor is a volunteer as well, and..." A muscle flexed in his jaw. "He tried to set me up with his daughter."

"Oh no."

I didn't think Owen had gone on a single date in the time I'd known him. He wasn't really open about it—what with him being such a chatty guy and all. He'd mentioned an ex-girlfriend from vet school that had gotten serious, but nothing else. I spotted a hickey on his neck once, and when I picked on him about it, he just shrugged and replied, "Hookup." It was hard to picture him having casual sex, but it wasn't unthinkable—a puzzle piece I was sure belonged if I could just turn it the right way.

If I just examined it...

And I did.

From. Every. Angle.

Even knowing that, no matter how it fit, casual sex wasn't a good fit for me.

"Yeah, he was persistent," he said.

"He tried more than once?"

Owen snorted. "I don't have a relationship on the radar, but some loud, pushy guy's mystery daughter doesn't appeal to me."

"Can't imagine why not."

"Shocking, I know."

"So, you show up and say you have somewhere else to go."

He nodded, and we ran in silence for a few strides. He looked straight ahead while I stared at him until he noticed. The wind shifted, sending his wintergreen scent my way.

When he raised an eyebrow at me, I suggested, "Wanna do New Year's Eve together? We could be each other's plus-ones."

He focused forward again. "You have a party you have to go to?"

"Work always throws one. I don't have to go, but I probably should. And there's all that mess with Sam... I really don't want to go alone."

Sam and his stupid, good-looking face with blue eyes and sandy brown hair. He was tall and leanly built. We shared an office, and that had been enough for our coworkers to make clumsy insinuations that we should date—no one had less finesse than fifty-year-old men. I would have probably agreed to a date with Sam, but he was obviously not interested.

Did that stop the old men from continuing to make comments about how good we'd look together?

No.

It was *very* uncomfortable.

Sam was my type, but when I caught myself thinking about men, it was Owen who was on my mind more than anyone else.

But when I'd hinted that he and I should go out, he said he had to take care of his dog. It was disappointing, but sometimes interest wasn't reciprocated. He was a great running buddy and he made me laugh, and that was enough.

Considering my string of failed past relationships, it was probably better to remain just friends. With my track record, he was bound to have a red-flag then I'd cut ties, and he wouldn't be in my life at all.

"Things still awkward there?" he asked.

I bobbed my head, considering how to answer. "I mean… I didn't like, throw myself at him, but I made it clear that I would like to have dinner with him, and he was definitely not interested. And the other guys at work haven't gotten any more subtle in suggesting that we date."

Falling into step behind me again, Owen waited until another jogger passed us. "You don't want me there. I'm shit at these things."

"I wouldn't have asked if I didn't want you there."

"Em, I suck at small talk. I don't dance unless I get way too drunk—"

"Hashtag, goals."

"I'm awkward at parties."

"You're awkward, anyway."

He smirked.

"Come on, man. I need some arm candy."

He coughed out a laugh. "I can go with you, but you don't have to come to this other thing with me."

"What?" My eyebrows shot up. "You're saying that you'll go to my party, but I'm not expected—no, *not invited*—to your party?"

"It's not like you're not invited, but you don't have to go with me."

"Um, weird, but okay."

We were almost halfway through our last mile as a comfortable silence settled with only the sounds of our footfalls on the frozen asphalt.

He came out of his shell once I got to know him, but he avoided crowds and people in general. It was out of character that he agreed to go to my work event. Honestly, it was peculiar that he'd willingly and without any real pressure on my end at all.

I studied him out of the corner of my eye. His eyes were deep-set under his dark brows. The straight bridge of his nose cut to his perfect mouth. His lips weren't overly full, but they were sharply ridged and defined. There was a soft knot where the joint of his jaw pushed against his skin. He was artistically beautiful. The ratio of his features would probably fit that "ideal" number for symmetry. And even though his face was distracting, I did not lose my train of thought as I watched him.

This time under my stare, he didn't look back. "What?"

"Why?"

"Why what?"

"Why will you go to my party, but I don't have to go to yours?"

"Does there have to be a reason?" He kept his gaze straight ahead. If I needed any more proof that he was hiding something, it was there when his jaw muscle jumped.

"For you to willingly, and with very little convincing, come with me and get nothing for it? This isn't, like, a movie I wanna go see. This is a pretty big social event." I waited for him to finally look at me. "And you *hate* people."

Dimples pressed into his tan cheeks as he smiled tightly. "It's not that big a deal."

"For some people, no. But for you, it's huge."

His eyebrows peaked like an inverted 'V.' "Can I take it back?"

"Oh no, you're committed now. I'm already planning our coordinating outfits. But you also have to spill."

"You know I don't actually have to do either."

"But you're going to."

Heaving a sigh, he puffed out a steamy breath. "You really don't want to know."

"Will I be implicated in a court of law or something?"

"I don't think I've broken any laws."

"Jesus, what'd you do, Owen?"

"I can't believe I'm about to admit this." He looked up at the gray sky as if it might hold the answers for him.

"Whatever you're about to say, there's no way it can live up to the suspense you're building."

He coughed another laugh, and with a challenging glance my way, he said, "My coworkers think I'm married."

The toe of my shoe caught on the path. I couldn't correct my balance, and I went down with my arms flailing. My gloved hands caught most of the impact, but there was a sharp bite of pain as my knee scraped against the asphalt.

"Shit," Owen exclaimed, turning and running back to me. "Are you okay?"

"Yeah, I just tripped." Rolling onto my butt, I shook out my hands. I looked down where the pain was emanating from my propped-up knee. There was a hole in my leggings, and the skin underneath was scraped, but it didn't look or feel very serious.

He lowered to one knee in front of me. "Didn't live up to the suspense, huh?"

He'd proposed to someone? What the hell... he was married?

"Shut up. You're married?" Why did I sound so angry?

"No." He slipped his gloves off.

My brain trudged through time at a slower pace than his. He wasn't married... but his coworkers thought he was. The unexpected anger was replaced with unexpected relief. Mouth open, I blinked at him.

"May I check your knee?"

I waved him off. "It's fine."

"You sure?"

"Yeah."

"I'd still like to che—"

I leaned forward and cupped his face in my hands. I could feel his heat, even through the layers of fabric. His deep-set hazel eyes snapped to mine. Our faces were close enough that the mist of our breaths met in the space between us like a swirling tangle of steam. It was the closest we'd ever been. It probably would have felt intimate with anyone, and it had nothing to do with the fact that Owen's face was only a foot from mine.

Letting go of him, I wrapped my arms around my thighs. "Why do your coworkers think you're married?"

# Chapter 2

## Owen

The cold from the ground seeped through the knee of my jogging pants. I mimicked her body language and leaned back, putting a more comfortable and normal distance between our bodies. I'd gotten used to the strange tingling sensations whenever we touched. She was so casual with contact, and she didn't even seem to realize when she was doing it. I could still feel the pressure of her hands on my cheeks after she'd pulled away, even through the thin layer of her gloves.

Slowly, it dissipated. The imprint of her fingers was like a memory slipping from vivid to hazy. Like the mist of our breath dissolving into nothing.

"It's a whole thing," I answered, knowing it wasn't an explanation. I hadn't told anyone but my friend Remi about the lie, and he'd been present at the birth of the idea.

Still, even he thought I'd gone too far.

And I didn't disagree with him.

Questioning my decision to tell my coworkers I was married had become a time-consuming pastime. It was a complete overreaction to an annoying problem.

In my defense, I hadn't actually told my coworkers; I'd told Mr. Maynard—a volunteer who would not stop trying to set me up with his daughter—who had told everyone else. The original lie had been small and completely forgivable. *"I'm sure your daughter's great, but I'm seeing someone."* An old faithful for the romantically uninterested. But the boisterous man would not accept the excuse.

While I was in Arizona visiting Remi, he'd joked, "You should tell him you went to Vegas and got hitched."

Laughing, I argued, "He'd probably give me a divorce lawyer's business card."

We'd laughed about it for the next forty-eight hours, but by the time I was home, it'd shifted from absurd to not totally ridiculous. I started troubleshooting possible complications. I'd always kept my work life and personal life separate in a major way, so I figured it couldn't be that hard.

It wouldn't hurt anyone.

But four weeks later, the story was still the main subject of conversation. And now I needed a way out of it.

I hadn't realized how curious everyone would be about my supposed wife.

*"What's her name?"* a coworker would ask.

I'd smirk. *"I'm not telling."*

*"What does she do?"*

*"Sales."*

*"How'd you meet?"*

*"I saw her for the first time and she saw me, then we became acquaintances."*

*"Why are you such a smartass?"*

*"Just lucky, I guess."*

Obviously, I needed to stage a divorce.

Em rolled her eyes. "Owen, why do your coworkers think you're married?"

I squinted at the tear in her pants, the exposed skin tender and pink. "I told Mr. Maynard I'd eloped, and he told everyone else."

She barked a laugh, and I couldn't help but smile. Her laugh always did that to me.

"That is a *huge* solution to a mildly annoying problem."

I nodded. "I regret it."

Throwing her head back, she cackled.

"It's not that funny, Em."

"You *regret* it? I can't imagine why, Owen. What the hell are you gonna do?"

"About?"

She rolled her eyes again. "Like, are you gonna be fake married forever?"

"It's complicated."

"Is that your relationship status?"

My lips pinched together. "I can't take you to New Year's Eve, unless..."

"I want to pretend to be your wife."

Heat rose up my cheeks. "Yeah."

"I'm gonna pass this time. Well, looks like I'm off the hook." She reached out her hand. "My ass is freezing. Help me up, please."

Clasping my fingers around her wrist, I stood and pulled her up with me. Her pulse beat a quick rhythm against the pads of my fingers. "I have a first aid kit in my car."

She shook her head. "Of course you do. If only you were as sensible about the stories you tell your coworkers. It's no big deal, though. I'll take care of it once I get home."

I nodded toward her leg. "Are you okay to walk?" Even if I treated dogs, I was equipped with basic first-aid training.

"I'm fine. So, how long have you been married?"

We started toward our cars. Her stride appeared mostly normal, with only the slightest favoring of her uninjured leg.

"We eloped four weeks ago."

"How romantic," she deadpanned.

"Yeah, we thought so." I flashed her a crooked grin.

Her cackle-like laugh echoed off the concrete of the overpass we walked under.

"Do you have a first aid kit?" I asked.

"I have stuff, it's fine."

"What *stuff*?"

"I don't know… I have band-aids and triple antibiotic."

"You need a full kit, Em. What if you get burned?"

"I try not to."

"Because that's how emergencies work," I scoffed. "You just try not to have them, and they never happen."

"It's worked so far."

"That's risky."

With a pointed look in my direction, she argued, "You have a fake wife."

I sighed, more than a little embarrassed.

"So, what's the lucky lady's name?"

"I've… I've actually never given her one."

Her eyes widened. Their striking shade of greenish-blue stood out against her pale skin, like the ocean against white sand. I was sure I'd eventually get used to them, but it hadn't happened yet.

"How have you not given your wife a name?"

"Anytime someone asks something specific, I evade the question."

"And they just accept that?"

"Well, not really."

"That sounds exhausting."

"It is."

We continued in silence, her full lips pursed in thought. "Obviously, you need to get fake-divorced."

"Obviously, but I'm waiting until after the holidays; otherwise, I think everyone will feel really bad for me."

"That's a good point. So, mid-January?"

I shrugged. The deceit didn't sit easily, but I'd dug the hole and I'd have to find a way out of it.

The wind shifted directions, and wisps of her light-blonde hair pulled loose from her ponytail and blew across her face. I wanted to brush it behind her ear. I'd gotten semi-used to my mildly intimate impulses when it came to her. They used to be more frequent when I thought she might like me back, but then she'd started talking about her new co-worker Sam, and it was clear she wanted to let me down easily before I shot my shot.

Even with that disappointment, I was so fucking into her.

The hour and a half I saw her was the best part of my week. By the time Friday night rolled around, I was antsy for Saturday morning because I'd get to see her. She made me feel completely comfortable, accepted, and like an awkward lovesick puppy all at once. But it wasn't her fault that I didn't know what to do with my hands whenever she was around. She made me laugh, and I loved making her laugh.

I just liked being around her.

The lawn that surrounded the parking lot where we met up was covered in snow. We both bent in standing stretches. The unexpected walk at the end was more of a cool-down than normal, and the cold was beginning to reach under my coat. I pulled my zipper all the way to my chin.

She sank down deep into a lunge. Her leggings hugged her ass, and I looked away, but not before noting the round curve of it.

"Okay, I'm done," she proclaimed after only a minute of stretching. "It's too cold out here."

Slipping my gloves off my hands, I put them in the pocket of my joggers. "Can I look at your knee?"

She flipped her hand dismissively. "Don't worry about it." But instead of tossing a wave over her shoulder like she usually did, she walked toward me. "Can I give you a merry Christmas hug?"

I stuffed my fists into my jacket pockets. "Is that a thing?"

"Only if it's cool with you."

My abs flexed in anticipation. "It's cool."

She wrapped her arms around my shoulders, putting her chest against mine. I slipped one of my arms around her back and cupped her ribcage. It wasn't that our bodies were pressed together, not really—it was a friendly hug and nothing more—but internally, my body went bright everywhere it met hers.

I had never felt chemistry with anyone else like I did with her, even if it was depressingly one-sided.

It sucked, but sometimes that was just the way it was.

Too quickly or not quickly enough—I wasn't sure which—she pulled away. "I hope you have a nice holiday."

"You too, Em. See you in a week."

"Actually, my family stuff bleeds into the twenty-sixth."

"Okay, so no run next week. I guess I'll see you New Year's Eve?" Hopefully, she couldn't hear my disappointment.

"We'll talk to figure out the details," she called over her shoulder as she walked to her car.

I jogged to my SUV. Reaching behind my driver's seat, I pulled out the first-aid kit from its spot. Emmeline was picking out a song on her phone when I tapped a knuckle against her window.

Her pale eyebrow lifted as she rolled down the window. "What's up?"

I held up the kit. "Here."

"You're kidding. I'm not taking your safety items."

"It's called a first-aid kit."

"I know."

"Just take it."

"What if you need it?"

"I'll replace it. Consider it a Christmas gift."

"But I didn't get you anything."

"Clearly, I'm more thoughtful than you," I joked.

Pinching her lips, she struggled against a smile. "You're going to make a fake woman so happy someday."

She reached a hand to accept the plastic case, and our fingers grazed in the transfer. Bright sensations lit up where her warmth met my cold, like summer night sparklers erupting under my skin.

"Merry Christmas," she whispered.

Taking a couple of steps backward, I made space between myself and her car. "Mm-hmm. Okay, it's cold as hell out here. Text me about the thirty-first."

"Bye." She gave a little wave before rolling up her window. I could clearly hear "All I Want For Christmas" by Mariah Carey from outside Emmeline's car.

Climbing into my vehicle, I watched her taillights disappear in my rear-view mirror.

# CHAPTER 3

## EMMELINE

"It was a good try." A smile pressed the deep wrinkles around Lewis' eyes even deeper. As my sales manager, it was his job to be supportive of my attempts to grow the business. Even if I kinda wished he'd join me in pretending my failed attempt never happened.

Chewing my lower lip, I grinned at his forehead. I wasn't embarrassed that I'd failed to land a meeting with the CEO of MacIntosh Construction. I was one of many salespeople who had tried to get a face-to-face with Bill MacIntosh in the limited time he was actually in the state of Michigan. I was one of many, who tried and failed. That was probably what I struggled with the most; the not standing out part, the not finding a way. "Thank you. Maybe next time, right?"

"Absolutely. Your uncle Dutch got a meeting with Mr. MacIntosh once, but he couldn't land the deal."

The tall industrial ceiling and polished concrete floors of the showroom made sound carry easily, and I wasn't surprised when my coworker Carl strode up. He was tall and thin, with a baseball cap always atop his head. I was pretty sure he was balding underneath it, but even with him being my next-door neighbor, I'd never seen him without his head covered.

"Talking about the white whale?" Carl leaned his elbows on the counter next to mine. I had to lean away from the waft of his cologne.

I nodded.

"Still not seasoned enough to give up?" His tone was just short of patronizing.

"I guess not." I tried to keep my mannerisms neutral while simultaneously preparing myself for him to make an overtly rude comment. I still hadn't puzzled out if he was really clever in the ways he spoke to me or if he was really dumb. Either way, the things he said weren't enough for me to file a complaint against him; besides, my almost exclusively male coworkers wouldn't understand.

"You really gonna try again?"

"If Dutch could get a meeting, it means they'll entertain the thought of moving business this way."

"What edge could you have over Dutch?"

I didn't clench my jaw, and for that, I deserved a medal. "That would be decided in the room. Can't lose if you don't play, but you can't win, either."

"Exactly!" Lewis exclaimed. "That's the attitude."

"Thank you." I stepped back to escape to my office. Maybe if I moved fast enough, Carl wouldn't get a chance to piss me off any further.

"Was it the same rejection email as last time?"

*Ugh, not fast enough.*

"I don't know. I didn't read it all the way through." I kept my irritation out of my voice.

He nodded. "It probably was the same letter everyone got. But you're right, at least you tried." His tone didn't match his words, though.

Lewis patted my shoulder like he might a kid who got a good report card. "You keep going for it."

My smile remained through sheer force of will. "I gotta get to work. I have a meeting with Spencer Micheals in an hour."

The split-second that Carl's face turned sour was worth the name drop. In our little corner of the world, Micheals' Building was the second largest developer of industrial buildings, second only to Bill MacIntosh. Dutch had worked tooth and nail to grow their business with McCarthy Rentals, and when he'd retired, their account was passed on to me.

A decision that hadn't gone without scrutiny, particularly from Carl Sanders. He'd gotten some of Dutch's clients as well, but not as many as Carl thought he should have.

"I noticed their numbers had dipped." He joined at my side, and our shoes echoed down the hallway to the offices.

I shrugged, but my stomach twisted. Their numbers had dipped... a lot. In moving clients around, they'd become my bread-and-butter until I grew my smaller accounts. But if the drop in business continued, I'd be in a rough financial situation.

It was okay this month, but next month might be a real problem. Until the smaller clients were built up, I needed their business to like, pay my mortgage.

I'd tried to schedule a meeting before Dutch actually retired, but Mr. Micheals was always too busy. I sent lunch asking to schedule a time, as well as leaving voicemails and emails. While it'd been difficult to get this meeting scheduled, they finally seemed to understand that I wouldn't take no for an answer.

"It's winter and holidays... down season, you know?" I answered.

"I could come with you. Maybe he'd be flattered to have both of us there."

"Oh, no thank you. I wouldn't want to put you out. You've got your own clients to worry about."

"I'd be happy to help you."

"Really, I'm good." My smile was beginning to hurt.

Carl shrugged. "Good luck, then."

I wanted to let him walk away—he was an ass—but my manners wouldn't allow it just yet. "And thank you for shoveling my sidewalk. You really didn't need to; I was gonna do it when I got home from my parents."

For the first time, he seemed genuine. "Don't worry about it. I was out there anyway. I love using that snowblower."

This time I didn't stop him when he turned and walked into his office across from the one I shared with Sam. Luckily, Sam wasn't sitting at his desk. At least I'd get to skip any uncomfortable interactions with him.

A few minutes later, I'd sent out the last couple of emails I wanted to before turning off my computer for the long Christmas weekend and heading out to the parking lot to my car. I'd even taken a few minutes to scroll through Owen's Instagram. Most of the photos were of dogs at his job, but he was in some of them. His handsome face, smirking as a puppy licked his nose was my new kink.

He was so hot... too damn hot.

For the past couple of months, he'd been the center of my fantasies. My hands ached to discover the contours of muscles under his skin. For a short time, I'd tried to distract myself with Sam, but it hadn't worked. I never imagined running my fingers through blond hair.

I flipped the hood of my coat down and shivered in my seat. The cold wind and nerves had tightened my shoulders up to my ears.

This meeting needed to go well.

"You can fix this," I assured myself, my stomach somewhere near my esophagus.

My phone buzzed against my thigh. The screen displayed a photo my brother Malcolm had taken of me and Mom last summer. The setting sun's golden rays filtered around our heads like a crown, with the lake splayed out behind us. It was one of my favorite pictures.

I tapped the phone button on my steering wheel to answer. "Hey, Mom."

"Oh, I didn't expect you to answer."

I snorted. "Why do you call if you don't expect me to answer?"

"I assumed you'd be busy. You are working today, right?"

"I'm actually on the way to a meeting."

"Well, I won't keep you. I wanted to confirm what time you'll be over tomorrow."

"Around six." If I could show up later I would, but Mom would throw a fit about missing Christmas Eve.

"That late? You can't come earlier? Did you wait until last minute again this year?"

"It's fine, Mom, just a little bit of wrapping to do." The unwrapped boxes buried my living room sofa. "Anyway, you're gonna have me out there for two nights, so I'm gonna relax at home for a bit beforehand."

"It's not exactly going to be stressful here. How much relaxation do you need in a day?"

I sighed. "Can you relax as easily at my house as you can at yours?"

"It's different."

"How so?"

"I've never lived at your house."

"Okay."

I resisted the urge to demand, *Where is this going?*

I was just stressed, and even if she was being demanding, I could be patient with her.

"You know I just like you here," she said.

"I know."

"What client are you meeting? Do I know them?"

I squinted against the brilliant light reflecting off the untouched mounds of sparkling snow lining the road. I pulled my chilled sunglasses from their spot on the dash. "Micheals' Builders."

"Oh, they were always good for Dutch."

I nodded, even though Mom couldn't see.

"What are you meeting about?"

Playing down the situation, I answered, "Just a little drop in rentals."

"Probably need to know they're still important. You should have booked this meeting before Dutch left."

"We tried, but they didn't have room in their schedules." I hated having to defend my abilities. I was good at my job.

She must have heard the irritation in my voice because she changed the subject. "If you're able to come out earlier tomorrow, I'd love that."

"I don't know if I'll be able to, but I won't be later than six."

Mom sighed with resignation. "I'll plan on that then. Do you want to practice your conversation with Mr. Micheals with me?"

It was a technique Dad did to combat his shyness. My memory was filled with images of the phone pressed between Mom's shoulder and ear while loading the dishwasher and talking with him.

"I appreciate it, but I'm good."

"Okay, if you ever need me, just call. I love you, young lady."

"I love you too, Mom. See you tomorrow."

Pressing the phone button again, I hung up.

In the final ten minutes of my drive, I envisioned the conversation I'd have with Micheals. Mom was partially correct; he likely just needed some attention. Something to prove that I'd treat him with the same attentiveness as Dutch had.

Just as planned, I arrived five minutes early. I parked and stepped carefully on the asphalt parking lot, the thin coat of ice and snow crunching under my boots. After tying my long black coat closed, I bent again to retrieve the fruit and chocolates basket from my back seat.

The walk into the industrial building that held their office was bitterly cold. Inside the vestibule, hot, dry air blew down from the ceiling.

When I entered the suite, an older woman wearing a green and red sweater and dangling snowman earrings directed me to take a seat.

"Thank you." I smiled. "Are you Meredith? I think we've spoken on the phone."

The older woman waved from behind her desk. "That's me."

"Pleasure to meet you." Cultivating a relationship with the rest of the staff was as important as my relationship with the boss. "You look very festive today. I love it!" I set the basket on the empty chair next to mine.

She beamed. "Oh, I am full of Christmas cheer! Just a couple more hours before I decorate Santa's cookies with my grandson. Santa is his best friend." She pointed to her chest. "I was his best friend, but now it's Santa."

I gasped. "That..."

The older lady checked over her shoulder for anyone else in earshot before she whispered, "*Bastard.*"

We laughed behind our hands, muffling the sound in the quiet office. The last of my nerves calmed. It was all going to get figured out; it'd be fine. Micheals just needed to get to know me better. Nothing I couldn't handle.

Our muffled laughter ended in sighs as the office door to her right opened. A white-haired man with a round belly pressed against his button-up shirt stepped out. I recognized him right away, even if it had been years since I'd seen him. With my warmest professional smile, I waited for his greeting.

"Ms. McCarthy, nice to see you." He held out his hand for a shake.

I stood and gripped his hand. "Mr. Micheals, thank you for making time for me." Then I bent to pick up the basket I'd brought. "Happy holidays!"

His eyes narrowed as he took the gift. "Merry Christmas."

It felt like a correction, but I was possibly hyper-sensitive. "Thank you."

I waited suspended in an expectant pause. When he didn't lead us into his office, I suggested, "Should we step into your office?"

His round cheeks pinked. "Do you think that's necessary?"

*Great start.*

"Um... I would rather chat with you uninterrupted."

"Alright then." He turned, and without glancing at his employee, he directed, "Meridith, join us."

My eyes snapped to the older woman, who looked down at her hands as she stood.

All the nerves that had left surged back. There was something under the surface, a deeper purpose for the drop in rentals than I'd originally thought. And I couldn't shake the feeling that it was my fault.

I paused outside the open office door, allowing Meridith to enter first. The older woman stood against the wall behind the desk, her cheerful sweater in contrast to the tight expression on her face. He set the basket on a filing cabinet before taking a seat behind his desk.

I forced my body language to appear friendly and professional as I took a seat opposite him. "I won't keep you long. I know you're busy, and I'm sure you're anxious to get home to your family."

He nodded curtly.

"We really appreciate your business, but we haven't seen any new rentals come through since last month. I wanted to touch base with you to see if there was anything I could do to strengthen our working relationship. I know you and Dutch go way back, and he's got big shoes to fill." I clasped my hands together to end their frantic gestures. They felt clumsy and larger than normal. Could hands grow spontaneously?

"Dutch is good people."

I let my affection for my uncle show on my face. "Oh, he's a gem."

"But he's not always a great listener."

My eyebrows pinched. "How so?"

"I told him you and I could not work together."

A queasy heaviness sunk into my gut. "Excuse me?"

"Ms. McCarthy—"

"Emmeline, please." Maybe I could turn the conversation around if we were less formal. I literally could not afford for it to do anything otherwise.

"Ms. McCarthy," he said firmly, "I'm a good Christian man." He waited, as if that would explain anything.

I blinked.

He sighed. "I avoid any appearance of evil."

"Okay... Good."

He must have seen that I was still confused because he pointed out, "You're unmarried."

"I... I don't know what that has to do with anything."

"I can't call you or have a meeting alone with you." He gestured toward Meridith, who clasped her hands against her thighs. She leaned against the wall as if she wished she could sink into it and disappear. "I told Dutch this wouldn't work, but he insisted that you'd be the best to help me."

My cheeks burned with a fine mixture of anger and embarrassment. "I am the best equipped to handle your account," I stated, my voice low and determined.

"I don't doubt your credentials, but it doesn't change my commitment to my wife."

"I would never—"

"I'm not saying you would."

"Then I'm very confused."

"The appearance of sin is just as sinful as sin itself."

His logic boggled the mind. Most of my clients considered themselves to be Christian men, so what was the problem exactly?

"Let me make sure I understand this... If I were married or a man, you would work with me?"

There was an idea taking shape, like the beginnings of a tornado, but I could not let it take form. That way would only lead to madness.

He held out his calloused hands. "Now don't go paintin' some picture where I'm discriminating against you."

*It's a bad idea. The worst idea. It will implode,* my more reasonable side explained to the unhinged part of me.

It was working, and I was getting a grip on the nonsense forming.

"Keep that talk up," he continued, "and I'll end this meeting now and call off all our existing business."

My panic flared. If he did that, my revenue would drop by half, making it impossible to pay my bills next month. I needed to buy some time until my other clients could make up the difference.

Maybe if I took time to breathe and calm the blood coursing through my veins, I could have formed a constructive thought. Maybe if I hadn't just had a conversation with Carl being condescending, I could have stopped the tornado from ripping through my brain. Maybe if I didn't feel like I had something to prove in this very male-dominated field, I wouldn't be willing to take such a drastic measure.

But it didn't really matter, because I said, "There's no need for that." He opened his mouth to speak, but I interrupted him. "I'm married."

*Holy shit, what have I done?*

"You are?"

"Yup."

*I am a fucking fool.*

"Your uncle didn't mention that..." A frown filled the wrinkles of his face.

"It's fresh... one of those kinda unexpected things. We've been friends for a while, and when we started dating it just worked... We eloped."

His bushy white eyebrows furrowed over foggy gray eyes. "What does he do?"

"He's a veterinarian."

*Yup, keep digging the hole. You're doing great. This won't blow up in your face at all.*

My mind buzzed with static as silence filled the room.

Meredith finally broke the tension. "Well, congratulations!"

"Thank you." My cheeks filled with a blush I hoped looked like the joy of a glowing newlywed and not that of a lying asshole.

# CHAPTER 4

## OWEN

**H**ey man, I'm gonna be in town on the 31st. Wanna hang? Remi's text was waiting when I walked out of work for the day.

*Sorry, I have plans,* I typed back.

*Really?*

*I do, on occasion, have plans.*

*Bullshit.*

*What are you doing in town, anyway?* I typed as I hurried to my SUV parked in its usual spot in front of the medical building. Closing my door, I was greeted with the interior of the vehicle being just as cold as the exterior.

*Told Mom I'd spend Christmas with the family, and... I might be moving back.*

*No shit, really?*

*Yeah, there's an opening at a vet in Grand Ridge. I'm interviewing.*

*Awesome, man. Good luck.*

*Thanks. What are these "plans" you claim to have?*

I rolled my eyes. *I have a donor's party, and then I'm meeting Emmeline for a party.*

*Oh, I get it now. Hot Emmeline.*

***There is only one Emmeline.***

***Well, isn't that sweet?***

***Shut up.*** I snorted before I threw my phone into the cup holder of the center console.

I pulled into my driveway twenty minutes later. When my phone buzzed again, I assumed it was Remi. I'd call him back. I was mentally and physically exhausted. Molly, my favorite vet tech, and I had a six-hour surgery removing a mass from a three-year-old Great Dane's side. The surgery wasn't expected to be intensive, but it quickly became clear that the original plan wasn't going to work. The fact that this dog, Journey, was one of the sweetest at work only made it a little more stressful.

I parked in my garage and pushed the button to close the overhead door. I looked down at my still buzzing phone and saw that it was Emmeline—and not Remi—calling. My plan to send it to voicemail changed. The photo of her smiling at the camera was one I revisited often. I'd snapped it on one of the rare times we grabbed a coffee after one of our summer jogs. She'd started the photo taking, insisting that we needed contact photos. Yet, it was weird for her to call. We texted on occasion but never called.

I pressed the device to my ear. "Hello."

"I did something so dumb." There was a high-pitched anxiety in her voice that had me sitting straighter.

With my hand still on the gear shifter, I prepared to drive to wherever she was. My dogs would be okay for an hour or two. "Are you okay?"

"I tried calling my cousin, but she didn't answer... and I'm freaking out."

"Alright, it's okay. Whatever it is, I can help."

"I just told my client I'm married."

My eyebrows shot up.

"Why the hell would I do that?" Her voice grew thin as it rose.

Had the guy come on to her? But that didn't make sense; guys must hit on Emmeline all the time. Did the guy go too far? But why would having a husband make him back off? It didn't matter that the scenario was completely fabricated, my knuckles went white from my tight grip on the steering wheel.

"I'm such an idiot. This is going to backfire so badly. What if he tells my uncle? Obviously, Dutch would deny it because *I'm not married!*" I jumped and pulled the phone away from my ear as she yelled. "I'm just a total fucking fool. Micheals wouldn't work with me without a husband, but my *lying* about one will be no big deal. And he'll tell everyone. All these contractors know each other. I'll never be able to live it down. It's hard enough to be the *only* woman they do business with, but now I'm the totally unhinged lady who made up a spouse."

Her stream of consciousness filled in as many blanks as it opened.

"Em, where are you?"

"Oh my god, I've just ruined my career." Her words wobbled, clearly on the verge of crying.

"Hey." I deepened my voice, gentle but firm. "Em, where are you?"

Her shuddering breath came through the speaker. "A Shell station parking lot."

"Where at? I'll come to you."

"I don't know... down the street from my client. I'm sorry, I shouldn't have called you all worked up like this."

"No, stay with me. Don't hang up. Just breathe."

Her breathing was shaky in my ear. I listened as it slowly grew more even, a gradual leveling. I waited a few more seconds with only her breathing filling the speaker. "Wanna tell me what happened?"

She sniffled. "I had a meeting with my new big client, and he said he couldn't work with me because I'm single."

"The fuck?"

"And I... I told him I was married."

We fell silent again.

"Because it seemed to work out so well for me?" I asked. It was a risky move because she'd either think it was funny or condescending. I really hoped she'd find the humor. Hurting her was the last thing I wanted to do.

She giggled, a little manically. "It was like I knew this was the worst idea, but I did it anyway."

"So, you're getting fake divorced in January, too?"

"I bet he'll love that."

"Fuck that guy, Em. You shouldn't have been put in that position in the first place."

"Are you saying it's justified?"

"I'm saying... I understand."

She sighed. "You really shouldn't make me feel better about this."

"Oh, I should make you feel worse?" I channeled my best scolding parent impersonation. "I'm not mad, Emmeline... just disappointed."

Her puff-like laugh split my face into a smile.

"I expected more from you. You should've known better," I continued.

Her laugh came in a bit too loud—the way humor hits harder when you're emotionally raw. "That's better."

"You feel terrible again?"

"The worst."

"Good." I would normally hang up at that point, but instead, I asked, "You sure you don't wanna hang out?"

"I'm sure. I'll let you go."

"Actually…" I stalled the inevitable hang-up, for selfish reasons as much as in hopes to keep cheering her up. She wouldn't have called if she didn't want a friend. "You wanna plan our New Year's Eve?"

"Uh, sure."

"I can probably be at your party around eleven. Where's it at?"

"That works, and it's at the Mills Center."

My eyebrows pulled together. What were the odds that her event and mine were at the same hotel?

"Really? What banquet room?" It wasn't the biggest coincidence, since it was one of the more popular event locations in the area.

"The Union."

The tension eased slightly from my shoulders since my party was in The Stadium. It'd be wiser to cancel, especially since the parties' proximity could lead to trouble. Normally, an excuse to avoid a social event could be a lot flimsier for me to bail, but I didn't want to miss out on a night with Emmeline, even if it was just as her friend.

So, I'd have to ensure no one saw me at the party with her, as unlikely as that would be. We'd just stay away from the doors. No big deal.

The other reason I should cancel was that I was too into her, and she didn't like me back. Self-preservation should have kicked in by now.

"Do you want me to pick you up?" I offered.

"I'll probably catch a ride there with my brother or something."

"Your brother will be there? I thought it was a work thing?"

"Work things are also kinda family things for me."

I nodded, even though she couldn't see.

"Is that okay?"

"Yeah," I answered, possibly too quickly. I was so used to compartmentalizing my life that I sometimes forgot other people didn't do the same thing. I'd probably end up meeting her parents and her famous Uncle Dutch I'd heard so much about.

"Oh God," she groaned. "I can't believe I did that. Why did I do that? I just keep reliving it."

I ran my hand down my face, the scruff on my jaw scrubbing against my palm. "It'll be okay. It's not gonna ruin your career. Can you pass the client on to someone else?"

"Yes, that's what I should have suggested instead of what I did. I panicked. He was talking about pulling his existing rentals... I wouldn't be able to pay my mortgage."

"I still don't get it. Why does it matter that you're single?"

Her voice came through with a heavier Northern accent. "He's a good Christian married man, and how would it look if he was making phone calls to an *unmarried woman*?"

I stared out my windshield, seeing nothing, my brain too busy processing her situation. It was too unjust to make sense of.

"I just wanna do my job," she whispered.

"I'm sorry, Em. That's unfair."

"Yeah... Anyway, I'll let you go. Thanks for talking me down. See you on the thirty-first?"

"Sure. I'll come dressed as arm candy."

She barked a laugh.

I smiled, imagining the back of her head pressed against the headrest of the car. I shouldn't want to make her laugh as much as I did; it shouldn't make me feel that good.

But goddamn, I loved hearing her laugh.

"What does that look like?" She giggled.

"Something tight and short."

"Oof, yes, please. You've got those nice gams."

I ignored the way her purred compliment made me stiffen. "I'll do squats beforehand."

"Can I watch?"

Alright, this was a little closer to flirting than we usually got. I could steer the conversation away to platonic or...

"You like that sort of thing? Watching?"

I could hear her doing the same calculations I had just done. Safe territory was still nearby, and she could bring us back there. "Only when I like the view."

My heart skipped a beat.

"Are you... objectifying me?" I should have taken a right back to platonic friendship, but it was too late. I had a stupid grin on my face as my tongue ran against the sharp point of my canine. I leaned against the driver's side door.

"Maybe a little."

*I like the view, too.* That was what I wanted to say, but was it too far? Fuck it.

"I like the view, too."

In the silence that followed, my blood rushed in my ears. My grip tightened on the steering wheel. It was only a second, but it stretched like taffy, only less sweet.

"Is it because I'm a fake-married woman?" she scoffed. "You like 'em off the market?"

I forced the disappointment out of my voice. "Maybe we're actually fake-married to each other."

"Oh my god, that would be hilarious. If I could pick a fake-spouse, it'd be you."

"If only I wasn't already fake-taken."

"I guess it's just fake-not-meant-to-be."

And just like that, we were back in the land of friendship. It was familiar and fine and completely disappointing. "Anyway, looking forward to seeing you next week."

"I'll be the one in the badass dress."

I was too busy wondering what that might look like that I almost missed her goodbye. "See ya, Owen. Thanks again."

"No problem," I replied after a long pause. "Talk to you later."

We ended the connection and I felt it sever. Resting my forehead on the back of my hand still gripping the steering wheel, I called myself all kinds of foolish. It had been years since I'd been this interested in anyone. There were women I'd liked, but nothing like this. Nothing like the high I felt for days after spending a couple of hours in Em's presence. Nothing like the nervous anticipation I weathered, knowing I'd see her in a few days.

I should have pulled back when I realized she didn't like me in return.

Because now, there was only one way this was going to go. I was too into her for it not to hurt when we went our separate ways. Maybe if she started dating this Sam guy, it'd be easier for me to slip away.

The idea rubbed me sore and brought up the memory of past wounds.

It had been almost three years since my ex-girlfriend, Natalie, left me for the best friend she told me not to worry about. The way I had *known* that it would happen, but I trusted her more than I trusted my gut. Three years since the emotional ups and downs—and let's face it, manipulation—destroyed my confidence.

But Emmeline wasn't Natalie.

And Emmeline wasn't even my girlfriend.

I just wanted her to be.

***

I was still thinking about Emmeline's voice a few days later while I was surrounded by the quaint Christmas cheer of my parents' house.

Including a few floral arrangements my dad always incorporated in the decorations, full of flowers from his childhood in Hawaii—Hibiscus, Birds-of-Paradise, and Anthurium.

When I arrived with my dog Indie, my dad pulled me into a hug, his arms strong and wirey. "Mele Kalikimaka!"

"Mele Kalikimaka, Hauʻoli Makahiki Hou," I returned, wishing him a merry Christmas and happy New Year and hugging him back just as tightly. My dad gave really good hugs. Pulling away, I turned to my mom. "Merry Christmas."

"Merry Christmas, son." She leaned into my side, and I wrapped my arm around her shoulder.

A few hours later, Indie looked at me with her tongue hanging out of her smiling mouth from her spot draped across Melody's lap. My sister sat with her short legs crossed at the ankles and her back leaning against the sofa. Absentmindedly, she petted the hound's head and neck. A small stack of gifts wrapped in paper grocery bags sat piled next to her.

"That dog is in heaven," Mom said next to Dad on the burgundy crushed velvet sofa. It was a match to the loveseat I laid across. They'd purchased the set when I was in middle school from an estate sale and never updated it. It was a combination of their environmental consciousness and not having spare money for a new sofa. So even though the furniture was about as old as I was, and the cushions were worn, they weren't planning to replace them.

"She's a good baby. Aren't you, Indie?" Melody cooed.

The dog's tail thumped against the worn carpet.

"You wanna come home with me?" she joked.

"You can't have my dog," I interjected.

"Come on, you already have so many."

"And they're all my favorites."

*Except for Maui*, I added silently. Our parents only allowed me to bring one of my dogs to their place.

She made a disgusted sound at the back of her throat.

"Aw. You're a sweet one, Owen." Dad gave me a crooked smile, so similar to mine. Mom always said it was the lopsided set of his mouth that really snared her. They met when she was stationed in Hawaii, and he followed her back to Michigan after less than twelve weeks of dating, and a short stint of a long distance. He claimed to never have regretted the move, even at the height of our winters.

Melody and I looked more like him, with our tan skin and black hair.

Back when I was a kid, we'd visit my grandparents every year in Lihue, but it'd been years since I'd been back. Mom and Dad would leave for their annual trip in a couple of days.

"Of course, he's sweet." Mom smiled at me.

I smiled back. "Thanks."

"Alright, I'm opening a present." Melody leaned for her stack of gifts. Her fingers brushed the edge of one of them, but she couldn't reach without disturbing Indie. I used my toe to nudge it farther away.

Melody glared as Mom and Dad laughed. I snorted, but I also sat up to push them back within her reach.

We opened our presents one at a time, chatting about why we picked a certain book or whatnot. Or I guess, they chatted while I mostly listened, per usual.

"Will they fit?" Mom asked.

I held the running socks I'd just opened to my feet. "Can't see why not." They were a higher-end brand, and she'd gotten me a similar pair the year before, which had become my favorite. "I could use another pair. Thank you."

"You're welcome." Mom's brown eyes crinkled at the corners as she smiled back at me.

It was a quiet Christmas with just the four of us and Indie. Mom and Dad made butternut squash soup and chili, and we ate while watching movies. We went for a walk in the late afternoon. The passing of time was emphasized by the bright lights wrapped around the tree, growing slowly brighter as the sun set outside the bay window.

But as I ate my second bowl of soup, I wondered if there had been a single minute Emmeline hadn't crossed my mind.

# Chapter 5

## Emmeline

The day after Christmas fell on a Saturday, and I was missing that weekly jog with Owen. And not just because scrolling through the same photos of him on Instagram wasn't nearly as satisfying as seeing him in person. In person, I could enjoy the journey his lips took from resting to that mouth-watering smirk. Or the way his focus made it feel like he saw my heart rate quicken. And it wouldn't just be the memory of his voice pouring directly into my ear, asking me if I liked to watch.

Ugh, I was liquefied; a puddle evaporating into steam by the forbidden radioactive fruit of him.

I kept opening our conversation, though we hadn't texted since the day before. It was just a brief *Merry Christmas*, and nothing flirtatious. I didn't miss him, not really. And if I did, it was because I enjoyed his company as a friend. Despite my intense attraction to him, that's what we were—just friends. He wasn't interested in me and that was okay; his company was enough.

Eventually, I would find someone else to drool over, and that person might even return my interest.

Until then... I'd secretly lust after Owen. Until then I'd replay the insinuated naughtiness of our phone call the other day in the back of my mind.

I needed to think about something else, and I needed a physical release from this... tension.

There was also the tension from my meeting with Micheals and the barely controlled panic and rage its memory gave me. When Mom asked how the meeting went, I insinuated that it was okay but there was room for the relationship to grow. I did not tell her that he thought I was married.

And he thought that because *I told him I was married.*

God damn. How was I ever going to get out of this?

I didn't know I was masochistic, but that was the only explanation for my behavior.

The kitchen door burst open, and Dutch's loud voice cried out, "Ho, ho, ho," just like he did every year.

Malcolm and I shared affectionate smiles for our favorite uncle. He patted his husband Tom's thigh before standing to greet Uncle Dutch, Aunt Lucy, and Laurie with our parents. Tom and I looped arms to join them.

Lucy slipped out of her bulky winter coat and looked cozy in her oversized chunky sweater.

Laurie's petite shoulders shrugged tight against the cold, despite the warmth the blazing fire in the living room created.

"Where's your coat?" I asked, my arms extended for a hug.

She shivered. "I don't like wearing them."

"She'd rather freeze her ass off," Aunt Lucy said as Laurie pushed past her mom to wrap her firm, thin arms around my shoulders. She pulled me down to press her cheek against mine. We rocked back and forth, both of us too excited to hold still. I understood why she lived in New York City instead of here, but I missed my best friend.

The commotion was hectic and joyful as bags of gifts for later were passed around and a jar of Dutch's famous molasses cookies as well. Christmas was yesterday, but this was my favorite part.

My mouth was full of a cookie when he asked, "How are my former clients doing?"

I held up my finger and chewed slowly, buying myself some time. "Great. A little dip with Micheals, but we had a meeting a couple of days ago." My smile was painted on a little too big and too still.

Over her dad's shoulder, Laurie squinted at my expression.

"He's a curmudgeon, but he'll come around. I had to work my ass off to get him. Real straight and narrow kinda guy. I said, 'damn,' in front of him once, and he didn't rent from me for a week." The natural volume of Dutch's voice broadcasted everything.

"Yeah, he seems a bit uptight."

"A bit." He laughed.

"Do you remember him saying anything when you told him I'd be in charge of his account?"

His bald head gleamed in the recessed lighting. "Not that I can recall." Wrinkles creased his forehead. "Why do you ask?"

"Nothing, just had a hard time getting a read on him."

Liar.

"He'll always be distant. The man won't come to my New Year's party because there's alcohol. But take care of him and he'll do business with you." He swung one meaty arm around my shoulders and pulled me to his side. "There's no one better than you, Emmie. You'll get him all figured out."

I didn't know what to do. On one side, I was riddled with guilt about deceiving my family and my client, and on the other, I really appreciated Dutch's trust. In all, I felt terrible.

Laurie wriggled her way around her dad. It was easy enough to pull me into the living room as everyone mingled around the kitchen table.

"What's going on?" she whispered. She was a few inches shorter than me, her face turned up to meet my eyes.

"Holy shit, you don't even want to know. I've got myself in it this time."

"You can't start there and not tell me."

"Okay..." I sighed. "I had a meeting with that client and he's, like, my major bread-maker." I double-checked that no one would wander into the living room with us. "He told me he wouldn't work with me because I'm not married."

Her already large eyes grew wider, making her look more fairy-like than usual. She opened her mouth to speak, but I cut her off.

"Without this account, my income would tank so fucking bad. I panicked and I lied to him... I said I was married."

The rigid way I'd been carrying myself was apparently catching because she went entirely still. Her mouth hung open, her eyes wide.

Slowly a smile grew on her face. Horror was replaced by shocked glee. "You did what?"

"I don't know how to fix this, Laurie." Somehow, I was beginning to smile, too. Maybe the absurdity of the situation was finally taking me to hysterical levels of humor.

"I... yeah, me either."

She was the first to laugh, her trill quickly cut off by a snort. Soon, we were laughing at the ridiculousness of my situation, clutching each other's arms so we wouldn't fall over. We were still catching our breath and wiping away our tears when Malcolm and Tom joined us.

"What's so funny?" Tom rested his head on my brother's shoulder.

"We'll have to do a toast tonight," Laurie wheezed.

"Keep it down," I hissed, checking if any of our parents had over-heard.

Malcolm shared a confused look with his husband. "Something to celebrate?"

"A new marriage always is."

My brother's eyebrows pinched closer together and his eyes nar-rowed.

Again, I checked how close our parents were. "I told an old client of Dutch's that I'm married."

"What the f—"

"Why on earth would you do *that*?!" Tom interrupted Malcolm.

Laurie and I fell into fits of laughter all over again.

"What's so funny?" Mom called from the dining room.

"Absolutely nothing," Malcolm replied, glaring just like Dad used to when we were kids. He turned to me and lowered his voice. "You have so much explaining to do."

Tom pressed his palm to Malcolm's chest. "Shut up and let her talk."

"Well, get your butts in here, it's time to eat," Mom called.

"We have time, go on." He swiped a dismissive hand through the air.

"I heard that, Thomas; and no, we do not have time. Get it in here."

Frustrated, he whirled away from us.

The traditional ham dinner we had ordered from a local restaurant steamed on the table as my family took their seats. After heating the dishes, we'd transferred them onto Mom's silver serving wear. The matching candlesticks held green tapered candles on a red table-cloth. Next to our white plates sat gold silverware and crystal wine glasses.

We all held hands as Dad said grace, seated at the head of the table in his quiet, solemn voice. His mostly silver head bowed, making the breadth of his shoulders appear even larger. His crystal blue eyes closed.

It was a scene made for a Midwestern dream.

Laurie and I shook with silent laughter, and neither of us could stop. Across from us, Malcolm glared, and Tom looked as if he would burst if he didn't get the rest of the story.

"Amen," Dad finished.

Dutifully, everyone repeated, "Amen."

Laurie swiped the pads of her ring fingers on the delicate skin under her eyes. Her short dark hair emphasized her narrow chin and high cheekbones. The tops of her ears even had soft points. She was a pair of wings attached to her delicate shoulder blades away from fairy cosplay. Her hair color came from her dad, but otherwise, she was a replica of her mom. Aunt Lucy dyed her light brown hair blonde and kept it long, but there was no denying the genetic connection between the two women. They were equally birdlike and petite.

The rest of the family was built broader. Even Malcolm's husband, Tom, was larger than the average person.

I had Mom's light hair and sharp features, though she made efforts to soften them with makeup. I, on the other hand, embraced the broad planes and angles of my cheeks and forehead. I looked like myself, and I liked how I looked.

"Food looks delicious, Vivian," Aunt Lucy complimented.

"Thank you. I asked them to try a different glaze on the ham than they did last year. Hopefully, it's as good as it looks." Then, with a warm smile, Mom asked, "How was the flight, Laurie?"

Mischief was bright on Laurie's face as she answered, "Good. It was a full flight, but totally fine. How was Christmas?"

If an expression could become nostalgic, that's how Mom's looked—misty-eyed and with a warm smile. "Beautiful. You know

I love this time of year, especially having my kids under the same roof." She let out a heavy sigh. "Being quiet with my family. It's just beautiful."

Malcolm and I shared a '*this lady*' look. For a woman who wanted a quiet time with her family, she flitted around and hardly ever sat down. There was always something else she could do. We had to pull out playing cards and board games to convince her to sit still.

"How was yesterday for all of you?" Tom asked.

Uncle Dutch drew his arms wide, encompassing his wife and daughter, his movements just as loud as his voice. "A relaxing day with my gorgeous family."

"Relaxing," Laurie scoffed. "The way this man celebrates, I'm surprised he didn't hire ten lords a-leaping." She shook her head, but Aunt Lucy gazed at her husband with doe eyes. "He hired a chef for breakfast *and* dinner, and we had to open our gifts from the middle of the living room just to get to the tree."

"Gifts are my love language," Dutch countered with a shrug.

"It's exuberant."

"I love you *exuberantly*."

"It's too much, Dad."

"Nothing is too much."

Heaving a heavy sigh, Laurie shook her head. "There's no reasoning with you."

"No, there isn't," my dad agreed.

Dutch guffawed. "Please, if it weren't for me, we never would have started McCarthy Rentals. I had to drag you kicking and screaming to get our loan."

A collective groan carried through us kids. The folklore of our fathers' business start-up was revisited regularly. But Dutch was prone to exaggeration, and Dad was never one to fight. Even though the story was always told as if he had to be thrown over Dutch's shoulders and carried into the bank forcibly, it was more likely that Dad had pointed out all the areas to be weary and Dutch had ignored them. But ultimately, they had invested equally and devoted all their efforts to the business' success. They had struggled. Their first few years had been lean, but somewhere around my tenth birthday, they started earning comfortable livings. And it had only grown since then.

It secured me a well-paying job—as long as I could fix the Micheals' situation—with room for advancement, something I really appreciated. Malcolm and Laurie thought I joined the business because I felt like one of us should, no matter how often I told them that I liked what I did. To them, it was dull work, but to me, it was a constant challenge of personalities and logistics.

"Yes, we all owe you everything, Father," Laurie said, her voice soaked in sarcasm.

At the head of the table, Dad flicked a smirk at his niece.

"We all made sacrifices, but it was worth it. Right, Luce?" Mom lifted her red wine.

A small smile, similar to her daughter's, in every way except for the lack of irony, pulled at Aunt Lucy's lips. "It wasn't always easy, but Dutch was always so sure."

Dutch grasped his wife's hand. "Enough confidence for the both of us."

In a mocking replica of her dad's display, Laurie took hold of my hand. I looked back at my cousin's pixie face in as close an approximation to Aunt Lucy's adoration as I could achieve. Tom concealed his smile behind his hand and Malcolm's shoulders shook with silent laughter.

"I see you two," Mom accused, but it was clear by the way she hid her face behind her wineglass that she thought we were funny, too.

# CHAPTER 6

## EMMELINE

My parents' home could have been ripped out of a Hallmark movie. The definition of holiday cheer, with a giant tree in front of two-story windows and a fire blazing in the fireplace. Malcolm, Tom, Laurie, and I had just separated from our parents. The crackle of burning wood welcomed us into the living room as the scent of pine and cinnamon comforted all our senses. It would have been wonderfully serene if not for Malcolm and Tom forcing themselves onto the same sofa Laurie and I had occupied. The sofa was only a three-seater, so the fit was tight. Each of us cradled a glass of red wine, balancing the contents to be sure we didn't spill on the white cushions.

"What the hell is going on?" Malcolm demanded.

The parents were settled around the table, but I still told my story in a near-whisper. Tom joined Laurie and me in shocked laughter to the point where my cheeks ached.

Adversely, Mal's face pinched in displeasure. "That's bullshit. That's discrimination."

"Well, it didn't feel very inclusive," I agreed.

"You couldn't send him to someone else?" Tom fanned his face. The heat must have been getting to him, too.

"Have you told Dad?" Malcolm was clearly in defender mode.

"No, I haven't told Dad! And don't you dare! I should have excused myself and had him reassigned, but I freaked out. I need this account to pay my mortgage..."

They all avoided my eyes. It wasn't such a funny story anymore.

"Uh," Tom began, obviously searching for a direction to turn the conversation, "you two going to Dutch's party?"

"I'm heading back to New York on the thirtieth. It's awkward as hell with Dad at social events and his," Laurie straightened her back primly and adapted a bad, posh English accent, "*possible suitors*. It's so uncomfortable. One of his friend's sons was in New York a couple of months ago, and he would not let it go until I agreed to take the guy out to coffee. It was... Oh my god, we could not drink our coffees fast enough. But whatever, he went back home and we're happily not keeping in touch."

"Fairy-tale love story," I mocked.

"I say this with nothing but love, but all of your parents are the most meddlesome of meddlers," Tom said.

"Dad's pretty normal." Malcolm shrugged.

"Aunt Lucy, too," I added.

"I think your mom and my dad make up for more than the difference," Laurie said. "I think Dad thinks if he sets me up with a guy in Michigan, I'll move back. Can you imagine his meddling if I wasn't hundreds of miles away?" One dark brown eyebrow lifted as she shook her head. "Anyway, what about you guys? Are you going to the extravaganza?"

But instead of waiting for a response, she proclaimed, "Oh my god!"

I jumped when she sprung for her phone with wide eyes, almost spilling the wine in my glass. "Did I show you the picture Dad sent me of the latest man vying for my hand in matrimony? Obviously, I'm sure this guy isn't actually looking to marry a total stranger, especially because the pic is a screenshot from his work, but goddamn, this man is hot, like... super effing hot.”

I snorted and answered her first question as she scrolled through her phone. “We will be attending the extravaganza. Every year I think it can’t get bigger, but then it does. But yeah, I was going to make an appearance and get the hell outta there, but now I have a friend who’s meeting me.”

She peeked up from her phone.

Concealing my regret, I shook my head.

*“You like that sort of thing? Watching?”* Christ, just the memory made me melt.

“We’re just friends.” I hoped I didn’t sound disappointed. “But I think people at work kinda picked up on my whole... I don’t know, Sam infatuation and having Owen there might be helpful.”

“You kids talking about Sam from the shop?” Dutch’s voice boomed through the room, filling the space as if to make room for his personality. “You got your eyes on him, Em?”

Laurie turned her phone screen-side down before her dad could see it.

“He’s a great asset to the company, really has an understanding of sales and growth. He’s a good-looking guy, too.”

“Sounds like a real catch, Dad,” Laurie drolled. “Are you and Mom considering polyamory?”

I nearly spit my mouthful of wine.

Tom wiped his chin with the back of his hand—clearly, it wasn’t just me.

Dutch blinked at his daughter. “What does that mean?”

Laurie shook her head. “Never mind.”

"I'm bringing a friend to New Year's Eve," I said in hopes that it would change the narrative around me and Sam, or rather, the lack of me and Sam.

His blue eyes brightened. "You aren't interested in him?"

Laurie rolled her eyes. "And neither am I, Dad."

"You don't know that. You should see this guy."

"He's not a mail-order. I'd really love for you to stop this. I don't exactly bemoan my spinsterhood."

"I thought I found you a good one," he argued.

"But alas, he is taken by another." Laurie draped the back of her hand across her forehead.

"Smart ass." He shook his head. Then to me, he said, "I heard a rumor that Bill MacIntosh might be in town in a few weeks."

"Really?" I sat up straighter. "So soon? He was just here a few weeks ago."

"That's the rumor. I'll let you know if I hear anymore."

I thanked him, already trying to think of a way to stand out to the local tycoon.

***

I was lightly buzzed while Laurie dozed, curled into the corner of the sofa a couple of hours later. *Home Alone* went ignored on the TV. I considered getting another glass of wine when my phone buzzed on the coffee table.

Reaching for it, I saw it was a text from Owen, and my stomach flipped. A picture of his beat-up running shoes filled my screen with the caption, ***These guys missed you today.***

Heat filled my cheeks and a smiled filled my face. ***Tell them I missed them, too.***

*They're also wondering how your holiday was.*

*It was really nice. How was yours?*

*Mine or my shoes?*

*Your shoes, of course. Did you get them anything nice?*

*I was going to give them my first-aid kit, but I already gave it to you...*

I laughed and rolled my eyes. *A new pair of laces would probably be more their speed.*

*If you wanted to tell me you missed me, you could just say it. I missed you, too.* My thumb hovered over my drafted text to send before I erased it.

Three dots showed up and then disappeared on my screen. A minute later, they came back, followed by his text. *I'm gonna put myself and my shoes to bed. Good night, Em.*

Disappointment took over the excitement that had just been there. *Good night, see you on NYE.*

"Who are you talking to?" Laurie's question made me jump.

"My friend Owen." I tried to be nonchalant, but now that I wasn't distracted by texting, I could feel the interest from her and Tom.

"Running buddy Owen?" Tom asked.

"Yup."

They shared knowing glances. They clearly had thoughts, but at least they didn't say any of them out loud. It was confusing enough to untangle the strings of what I knew Owen and I were with what I wanted us to be.

*Just friends* had security, it was reliable. Romantic entanglement had a way of being messy. It was possible that I had a history of cutting and running at the first signs of a red-flag, but that in itself was reliable.

And in this case, disappointing.

# CHAPTER 7

## EMMELINE

Four days could feel like an eternity. It took four whole days, but then it was New Year's Eve. My interest—*obsession*—in Owen might have been a problem I didn't know how to cope with. I was jittery with excitement and nerves. And even though I didn't expect him to show up at Uncle Dutch's party for another couple of hours, I still kept checking the hall's entrance.

It was a bit much for a *just-a-friend* non-date.

Malcolm, Tom, and I had arrived almost an hour before, and we had been dancing and drinking ever since. On the drive from my place, we listened to pop music in our fancy clothes, singing along very poorly. We made up the three worst voices in the Northern Hemisphere. Half of every song disintegrated into laughter at failed notes or lost pitch.

My watch displayed a text from Owen. **At party number 1. See you in an hour.** I texted back a thumbs-up emoji, even though I knew I'd watch the next sixty minutes tick by at an extra slow rate.

He was right on time for the itinerary, of course. He was a schedule-conscious, prepared-for-any-eventuality kind of man, proven by the first-aid kit that now lived in my trunk instead of his.

"What are you smiling at?" Tom asked before plopping a stuffed mushroom into his mouth. He towered over me in my two-inch heels, which put me just under six feet.

"My friend texted, and he's getting to his party. It's funny how anti-social he is, like he's just getting out for the night."

"What's funny is you claiming he's just a *friend*," Tom replied dryly. "I haven't seen denial like this since I told my high school girlfriend the pictures of Jake Gyllenhaal in my locker were because I really admired his acting."

"I'm not into him." I laughed to cover my lie.

I assembled cheese atop a cracker from his plate while balancing my half-full glass of champagne in my other hand. My stomach was pleasantly warm from the alcohol and my lips were in the beginning stage of numbness.

"Okay, babe." Tom clearly didn't believe me. "Why aren't you two spending the whole night together?"

"Uh..." I hadn't anticipated the question, and my fizzy brain couldn't think of a vague explanation quickly enough. It was one thing to tell them my lie, but I didn't want to spill Owen's. "It's like... a whole story."

Tom tipped his head, his salt and pepper hair catching the dim overhead light.

"What's a whole story?" Malcolm asked, joining us. He sipped from the glass of water in his hand, slipping his other arm around his husband's waist.

"Something to do with her *friend*." Tom lifted his bushy eyebrows to emphasize how much he didn't believe the relationship was platonic.

"Tom, sometimes a straight man and woman are just pals," Malcolm defended.

I beamed at him. "Thank you."

"You're welcome. Now, tell me this story about your soon-to-be boyfriend."

Tom's laugh burst from his chest like a bass drum.

Sighing, I tried to move the conversation away from Owen's secret. "Okay, yes, I'm... I like him so much, but he doesn't like me, and that's okay. I've had enough lackluster relationships to know when something just isn't going to work."

They shared a look.

"Has he told you he's not into you?" Malcolm asked.

"No..." I looked over my shoulder and lowered my voice. "I mean, there was a... conversation last week that has me... I don't know."

"You should say something."

"New Year's kiss!" Some of Tom's champagne sloshed over his hands as he clapped to emphasize each word.

I rolled my eyes. "Have you forgotten...? I'm married."

Malcolm rolled his eyes. "Sadly, no, I haven't forgotten. I've been waiting for a frantic phone call from Mom demanding if I knew."

I downed the remainder of my drink to combat the spike in my blood pressure. "So far the cat is still in the bag."

Malcolm's lips pinched.

"Okay." Tom swiped his hand through the air as if wiping our conversation off a chalkboard. "Back to your... not-a-date. What aren't you telling us about Owen?"

It was too much to hope that Tom could have been distracted. "It's not my story to tell."

"So you're not going to tell us?" he groaned.

I shook my head. "And I don't want you to ask him. I shouldn't have said anything."

"I mutant!" Tom exclaimed.

Malcolm and I shared confused looks.

Malcolm grinned. "Do you mean mutiny?"

"Yes!"

I was clearly not the only one feeling the effects of the champagne. We were still a huddled group of laughing goons when Dutch and Sam walked up.

Sam stood between me and my uncle. He wasn't as tall as Tom, but just barely shorter. Sam's navy suit fit his tall, lean frame perfectly—all crisp lines and long seams. The gold tie around his neck matched my metallic party dress.

He looked so goddamn hot, but it just made me wonder how Owen would look tonight.

"Look at you three!" Dutch exclaimed, his voice booming over the party's volume. "Looking sharp, enjoying yourselves. This is my favorite part of every New Year's Eve."

My tipsy heart gushed with sentimentality for my sweet-hearted uncle.

"Sam, this is my nephew Malcolm, and his husband Tom."

"Nice to meet you, I'm Sam." He reached out a firm handshake to both of them, which was received with heart-eyes. I totally got it; the man filled out a suit nicely.

Gesturing, Dutch turned his attention to me. "Of course, you know my beautiful, exquisite, intelligent," I tried not to cringe that intelligence came third, "go-getting niece, Emmeline."

"Why'd you stop? I thought the ball was just gettin' rollin'." I rolled my eyes.

Sam chuckled. "Yeah, we've met. How are you tonight?"

"I'm well, thank you. You look debonair." It was only reasonable to point out the obvious.

"Thanks. You look..." he did a very flattering eyebrow raise, "amazing."

I felt amazing in my gold, mid-thigh cocktail dress. The fabric made my pink tones glow as if sun-kissed which, in the middle of winter in

Michigan, it was not. It had a wrap front that V'ed between my breasts and upwards between my legs. I'd chosen a smoky eye done in bronze and red lips. I wore gold sparkling nylons. I even changed the band on my watch to a rose gold. My normally laid-back look would come back on January first while I slept off the hangover I was sure to have. But tonight, I looked like a female Midas—assuming Midas was gold and not just everything he touched.

It might have been too far, but every time I caught a glimpse of my reflection, I was sure I pulled it off.

"Thank you. It's fun to dress up." Then, because it felt like he and I were being scrutinized by the rest of our group, I turned the conversation to Dutch. "I was surprised we weren't in The Union."

"The invite list grew past capacity, so they had to move us to The Stadium."

Malcolm guffawed. "Had to rent a stadium for all your friends?"

Throwing his arms wide, Dutch encompassed the large room of people. "What can I say? I'm a well-liked man."

"At least your booze is." I waved my empty glass through the air. His large belly bounced with laughter. "Speaking of, I'm going to get a refill. But truly, Uncle Dutch, you've outdone yourself again. It's beautiful."

If 90s country glam were my aesthetic, this would be the height of sophistication. Judging by the pride on his face, it was everything he wanted it to be. And for that, I was happy. As if to commit to the look entirely, Dutch wore a bolo tie with his black suit, the two strings connected around his neck by a miniature sterling silver excavator.

"Thank you, sweetheart. It's always a fun night."

"It is. I'm off to the bar."

"I'll join you," Sam offered.

"Great."

He fell into step behind me. I looked over my shoulder to catch the reactions of my family members, knowing it was in their nature to make something out of nothing, but instead, I caught Sam taking in an eyeful of my ass.

He had the decency to look embarrassed and train his attention straight ahead.

*Huh? That's interesting.* But I shrugged it off. I'd ogled him plenty. There was a time I would have been happy to go on a date with him, but that ship had sailed, leaving port when I didn't even know it was scheduled for departure.

He seemed like a nice enough guy, though.

But I was too busy with feelings for Owen, even though it was unclear if it was a fruitless cause or not. Maybe that whole conversation was a preamble to a purely physical relationship, which I wouldn't do. I haven't been capable of maintaining the necessary emotional distance needed to sustain a physical relationship in the past—it just wasn't me. That was Laurie's thing.

It didn't take long to weave to the bar with Sam in tow, and we both waved to Carl when we passed him and his wife, Trisha. She lifted her eyebrows when she took in Sam. She'd be watching through her front window to see if he came home with me tonight.

I leaned my elbow on the small slice of the counter as we waited for the bartender.

"Are you having a good time?" I asked. Sam stood slightly behind me, so I had to twist at the waist to face him. The distance between us was a little closer than what would have been considered polite.

He nodded. "I am. Is it this big every year?"

"This is the biggest year. When next year comes around, that will be the biggest year."

The bartender took our orders, and we waited for the drinks to arrive. I fished for something else to talk about that wasn't work-related, but my brain pulled up nothing.

Even with Owen's quiet tendencies, he could always find a way to keep a conversation going.

I really didn't know anything about Sam, and that wasn't for lack of trying—the man was a steel trap.

"You really do look amazing tonight," he said quietly, a new purr in voice.

I blinked, my mind sputtering for a moment. "Thanks... you do, too."

A month or two ago, I would have been ecstatic about the compliment, but now, I just wished it was Owen's voice, low and near to my ear.

The bartender returned with our drinks, and we stepped back, a glass of water in one hand and a champagne flute in the other.

Either it was the lighting or there was a blush creeping up Sam's neck. "Would you like to dance?"

"Sure." I pointed to my glass of bubbling golden liquid. "Can we do it after I drink a little of this? I'll spill it all over the place otherwise."

Maybe in a few more sips, I'd be able to imagine what we'd talk about during that dance. I had a hard time picturing Sam dancing to an up-tempo beat. His movements were too... wooden.

"Yeah."

Okay, he was definitely blushing. Where was this coming from, exactly?

"Great." I gave him my friendliest smile. Nodding in the direction we'd come from, I led the way back to our group. "You coming?"

He swallowed a gulp of beer before nodding.

We had to stop and chat with a coworker on our way. But when we approached Tom, Malcolm, and Dutch, there was someone new standing with them.

I recognized the man's strong shoulders filling out a light gray sweater, which looked soft to the touch. The sweater, not the shoulders—those looked rather firm. I'd imagined touching them for almost a year. He was the shortest man in the group, probably about an inch shorter than me in my heels.

Looking over his shoulder, hazel eyes swept from my golden heels, up my sparkling legs, over my body draped in metallic fabric, and finally landed on my face. He blinked before his eyes widened. His beautiful artistic mouth opened in an "O".

My mouth hung open in equal surprise, a pleased smile spreading on my face. "Owen."

"Wow. Em." Owen shifted toward me, his hand reaching for mine, but gripped my waist when he realized my hands were full of beverages.

"You're early." My face split into the widest grin. I could practically see my own eyes sparkling.

"What are you doing here?" He was close enough that I could smell the wintergreen on his skin and something else. Something that must have been just him.

The pad of his thumb brushed against the fabric of my dress just under my rib cage. It was a direct line to my heart rate, a tap on the accelerator. I hadn't realized my body was asleep until it woke up from his proximity.

On the balls of my feet, I swayed toward him—a shift in my balance. My chest opened like the heart thudding against my rib cage needed to be closer to his.

Through the haze of alcohol and the effect he had on me, it took me a while to comprehend his question, which tickled warning bells in the back of my mind.

"Dr. Kauahi." The tentative way Dutch spoke was so out of character, it distracted me from the warmth of Owen's fingers. I looked down at the hand on my waist. On the ring finger, I saw a golden band.

A cold shiver spread down my spine.

"Do you know my niece?" Dutch asked.

I built the scenario backward. Owen standing next to Dutch, a wealthy man who recently retired with new-found time on his hands—time he might spend volunteering at a dog shelter he made charitable donations.

If anyone could drive a person to lie about their marital status, it would be Dutch.

Owen wasn't early.

This was his first stop.

# CHAPTER 8

## OWEN

I held perfectly still. Mr. Maynard's nephew and his husband—who I'd just been introduced to—exchanged confused looks. Mr. Maynard's large stomach bounced as he cleared his throat in surprise. There was a fourth man holding a long neck of beer just outside the group, who looked equally confused at my hand on Emmeline's waist.

The touch had been unconscious. It wasn't until she was warm and firm under my palm that I realized what I'd done and in front of who. *Mr. Maynard.*

I couldn't pull my hand back, not now that she was finally right there, her bright eyes sparkling at me. Her smile was full of welcome and something else I didn't have words for, but it made my chest expand. It had been too long since I'd seen her outside of my phone screen, too long since I'd breathed the same air as her.

"Dr. Kauahi, do you know my niece?" He pronounced it closer to *kow-ah-hee*, instead of my name's actual pronunciation *kowah-hee*, but I wasn't interested in addressing it at the moment.

Her pupils dilated; the large black circles were surrounded by vibrant green-blue. The muscles that had lifted her lips in greeting lost all tension as her jaw hung slack. Under my hand, her ribs tightened with a gasp.

My floating feeling was quickly replaced with a sinking sensation in my stomach. I needed to do something different with my hands. I grabbed her drinks and felt like a total idiot just holding them.

I flicked my head around, looking for somewhere to set her beverages, when she recovered from her shock.

She grinned at her uncle. "Yeah, we're friends. We go for runs together. How do you know Owen, Dutch?"

It was a casual question, but I had the feeling that she understood something I was still piecing together—a reality I didn't want to be true. But I was pretty sure I'd watched the second all the pieces fell into place, and she had figured everything out.

It would be fine, though. We'd make it clear that we were friends, and I wasn't the date that was meant to show up. I'd stay for a short time and then leave.

Any misconceptions that she was my mysterious wife would be laid to rest.

Maybe she'd even spend the rest of the night with the animated Ken doll who'd followed her to the group. The one who looked at her like a lost puppy.

Even if she didn't, that would be the way her night played out in my mind. Instead of ringing in the new year with this gorgeous woman I thought about constantly, I'd go home. I could take Bandit for a jog in the freezing cold, anything to occupy my mind from thinking about the way her dress plunged between her perfect, petite breasts and draped over her hips. Anything to stop me from feeling that it might actually work out better for her if I just left.

I had to assume that the Ken doll was Sam. She'd described him once as tall and a Hemsworth bother look-a-like. An apt description, really.

Sam was the guy she wanted anyway.

"He's a volunteer at work," I answered, hoping it would move the conversation along, finally setting her drinks on a nearby table as if it wasn't a completely awkward thing to do.

"Oh, that's great." She nodded a bit too aggressively, her head bobbing with more enthusiasm than volunteering had ever received. "Owen always speaks so highly of the shelter. I bet you have so much fun there and get to hang out with all the dogs. I bet—"

"Emmeline," Mr. Maynard interrupted her gently. I was too aware of her stiffened stance and the controlled rise and fall of her breathing.

She flipped a golden tendril over her shoulder and shifted her weight from one foot to the other. She smoothed her palms down her hips.

I swallowed, but otherwise didn't move, and even that felt like a proclamation of guilt.

He tilted his head as he spoke with more hesitation than I'd ever seen from him. "Micheals reached out to me a couple of days ago... He left a voicemail."

Under the dim light, the color drained from her face. Over her shoulder, Tom's eyes grew wide and Malcolm scrubbed a hand on his jaw. I would be surprised if he was even breathing.

"He wanted to congratulate me," Mr. Maynard continued. "I thought maybe he meant to call someone else, but... he mentioned a veterinarian." He narrowed his eyes at me in an expression of curiosity and skepticism I wouldn't have believed he was capable of, especially since he was always so jovial. "Are you married to Dr. Kauahi?"

Emmeline and I locked eyes.

Hers were wide and pleading.

I tilted my head in silent question.

The nod of her head was subtle.

For the briefest moment, I weighed the foolhardiness of proceeding and the deeper hole we would dig by tying her lie to mine. But there wasn't much to do about it. Our deceits lined up too closely; to deny hers would deflate the tentative reality of mine and vice versa.

My hand was steady as I took hers—the years of surgical training kept it from shaking as adrenaline coursed through my veins. Her fingers were like ice as I interlaced our hands. My free hand went to rest on her hip just like it had a few moments before. It curved around her and settled into its new favorite place. Her palm pressed into my chest—it seared an imprint onto my skin, an electric charge from her palm through my sweater that I'd wear forever.

I needed to remember that her touch wasn't as real as the way it made me feel.

"It was…" I tried to find the right word, "unexpected."

It skated between reality and lies, and she gushed a breathy laugh.

At the edge of our group, Sam took a large step back before turning to walk away.

I let myself take her in, in a way I couldn't usually. The long slope of her pale eyebrows, which were darker tonight than usual. The oval shape of her bright eyes. The bold, high cut of her cheekbones. The rounded tip of her nose. Her upper lip was slightly slimmer than the pouty lower one.

I let the heat I felt for her burn through my gaze. It might not look like love to anyone watching, but it wouldn't look like friendship, either.

A soft pink blush rose on her skin.

Her fingers had warmed as I pressed them to my mouth.

"Did you know?" Mr. Maynard asked Malcolm and Tom.

Tom sputtered, but Malcolm stated, "Yes."

She let out a sigh, as if some of the weight on her shoulders had passed to her brother. I couldn't have asked for a more supportive fake brother-in-law.

"Why didn't you say anything?" Mr. Maynard turned his attention back to Emmeline, then to me. "Why didn't you come for Christmas?"

We pulled apart, our hands still clasped, like two people facing imminent danger together.

"It..." She shrugged, "it was ours. Our secret. We weren't ready for everyone to know."

He blinked his watery blue eyes. "Well, goddamn!" he exclaimed loud enough that the groups nearby turned toward ours. "Congratulations! Do your parents know?" His arms extended toward her and when she went to hug her uncle, cold replaced her body heat at my side.

She bit her lip. "Not yet."

"Mom is going to flip," Malcolm said into his glass of water.

"Of course not!" Mr. Maynard shook my shoulder. I hardly moved, not with my feet planted as they were. "When she gets to know Dr. Kauahi—I'm sorry, *Owen*—she'll be thrilled. We're going to throw a huge reception!"

"Uncle Dutch, don't go making plans—" Emmeline tried to tamper his enthusiasm, but the big man was on a roll.

"Nonsense! My favorite niece is married! We're already drinking champagne! There's so much more to celebrate! Owen, let me get you a drink. We need to toast!"

"I'm driving, so only the toast for me." I needed to get a grip on this new enthusiasm before it got out of hand.

"No, no, you two can have my and Lucy's room in the hotel. We'll find a ride home."

"That's so sweet, but there's no need for that," Em said.

"I have to let my dogs out but thank you for the offer." I felt only gratitude for my pack of dogs.

For a brief, glorious moment, Mr. Maynard looked disappointed, but then his face lit up. "Okay, I'll find you two a ride home so we can properly celebrate."

"My car—" I tried, knowing it was pointless.

"Don't worry about it. I'll pay someone to drive it home for you, or I can pick you up and bring you back here tomorrow. We'll figure it out."

That was it.

There was no stopping this man.

The night just got so much longer and much more complicated.

"I'll take them home," Malcolm offered.

Relief loosened the tension in my shoulders—at least Em and I would be able to go to our separate homes. I'd call her tomorrow and we'd work out how to pull this off. Maybe she could make an appearance at the shelter's open house next weekend.

Mr. Maynard craned his neck to look over the scattered groups of people. "Where are your parents? We can't toast without them. I'll go make the announcement!"

"Announcement?" My racing mind stalled.

"No, Uncle Dutch—" Emmeline reached for Mr. Maynard's forearm, but he was already heading away from us.

"Dutch," Malcolm called after his uncle's back, but then he turned to Emmeline. "I'll try to stop him."

"Thanks."

Tom's mouth hung open at his husband's disappearing back. "I'll go look for your parents." Turning, he walked away, leaving me and Em alone, holding hands in the middle of a large party. I should probably let her hand go, but instead, I ran my thumb across her knuckles.

The past few minutes were convoluted in my memory. Working backward, I tried to figure out how I got to this timeline—the one where I was "married" to Emmeline.

"What just happened?" I asked, mostly to myself.

"Um, I got caught in my lie," she whispered. Our heads tilted closer to find privacy in the middle of the crowd. Her mouth was close enough that the puff of her breath carried the faint, sweet smell of alcohol. "And you did me a solid—"

"Em, I got caught in my lie, too. How was it going to look if I denied it?"

"It wouldn't have happened if I hadn't lied to someone who knows my family."

"Would you have told him that if you hadn't known about my lie?"

She leaned back on her heels, pursing her lips. They were a tantalizing shade of red, and I was having a hard time not staring at them.

"I don't think you would have," I continued. "It's a crazy thing I did and clearly, it's contagious."

She laughed, looking down at her feet, her forehead pressed against my shoulder. "Stop making me feel better."

"Stop trying to feel bad."

Lifting her head, she looked at me through her eyelashes. "Well, looks like we are roommates for a couple of weeks."

I startled, straightening my spine. "What do you mean? Why would we live together?"

"Are we the type of married couple who doesn't? Like, if we're going to sell this, we need to be convincing."

"But who's going to check where we live?"

"My coworker is my neighbor, and he's here tonight."

I snorted and shook my head. "Well, that'll do it."

She looked down at her shoes. "I know... I'm sorry."

My hand slipped around her back as my thumb massaged a small line along her spine. "No, it's okay. You've got nothing to be sorry about. Come to my house. We'll figure it out."

I ran through a mental checklist at the realization that Emmeline was going to see my house. Had I left anything embarrassing out at home? Anything I wouldn't want Emmeline to see? But I knew I hadn't, or I risked Venice chewing it up. Even inside his kennel, he might find a way to drag things into it. No, my house was as spotless as a house could be with five dogs—one being a St. Bernard and another a Husky—but it was still a small house with five dogs living in it.

I wasn't one for guests.

There were logistical issues I had to explain. The sleeping arrangements weren't ideal.

"Why your place and not mine?"

"I have five dogs."

"Five dogs?!" she sputtered.

I tugged our still joined hands and closed the little space between our bodies. "Darling... you knew that."

I soaked up her heat as she pressed her forehead into my chest and laughed. She smelled so good, like coconut.

The proximity of our bodies recalled fantasies and dreams that were always a thin layer beneath the surface of my thoughts. Even though I wanted to hold her fully against my chest, I didn't.

I needed to remember that this was all a lie.

"Why do you have five dogs?" Her mouth brushed my ear.

I shrugged. "They're good dogs. They weren't getting adopted because of behavior or medical reasons, so I took them in."

She sighed and rested her head against my shoulder. "That's really sweet."

I swallowed, not knowing what else to do. What was I supposed to do when the woman I was infatuated with was still holding my hand and there was so little space between our bodies?

"So... Mr. Maynard is your uncle?"

She pulled away and looked up, the ocean depths of her eyes swimming with humor. "Actually, he's Mr. McCarthy. His first name is Maynard, but he goes by Dutch."

Even though she'd explained as clearly as possible, I was still confused. "Why does he go by Dutch?"

She lifted one shoulder. "Because his name is Maynard."

"What kind of name is Maynard?"

"My grandma's maiden name."

"Because he's your uncle."

"Yes."

"Oh, Em, there you are," a woman said from behind me.

When I turned, I saw an older version of Emmeline. Her hair was swept up in a sophisticated twist and her clothes were sedate. She was more petite; whereas Em had a body that looked strong, this woman was all soft edges.

"Mom—" Em released my hand and took a step toward the other woman.

"Sweetheart, who's your friend?"

"This is Owen. But Mom—"

"Young lady, that was hardly an introduction—"

Tom approached with a large man in his fifties.

"Dad," Em said to the stranger. "Mom, just listen—"

"Can I have your attention?" A loud voice carried through the speakers that had been playing a 90s country ballad just seconds before. All eyes swept to find the source—all except mine and Emmeline's. Hers found the floor and mine watched as her shoulders sagged.

I rubbed the back of my neck and looked to the edge of the dance floor where Mr. Mayn—no, Dutch—stood. Malcolm grimaced just behind his uncle.

Tom's mouth hung open. He shared a horrified look with Emmeline that I only noticed out of the corner of my eye. I was too busy watching the man with a microphone about to implode a very fragile ecosystem.

"Now, you all know me... I'm a sucker for a romance."

The gathered group broke into an "Aw." If I wasn't at the center of the implosion, I probably would have found it endearing, too.

"My niece Emmeline, the most lovable person ever to live—"

I puffed a humorless laugh; he was right.

"Well, our beautiful Emmeline has found a whirlwind romance."

Weighing the situation, I considered the near future as quickly as possible. Dutch would pronounce us husband and wife, and there would be an aftermath.

I took Emmeline's hand again. Regardless of the misguided decisions that got us here, we were tied together in this lie. I pressed her chest against mine—she felt just as firm and satisfying as I'd imagined—and my fingers splayed against the small of her back. Her mother startled.

With Em's face inches from mine, I whispered, "We can do this."

In the microphone, Dutch proclaimed, "I just found out a few moments ago that she is married! Everyone, help me welcome Dr. Owen Kauahi to our family!"

Individuals in the crowd turned in circles, searching for us like particles warming up.

But for a few fleeting moments, I held her. For a few fleeting moments, I was a man with my arms around the woman who preoccupied all my thoughts. Just a few moments before the bubble popped.

"What did he just say?" Em's mom asked.

Em took in a deep breath, and I felt her breasts lift into my chest. Exhaling, she stepped back. Her shoulders squared and still holding my hand, she said, "Mom, Dad, I'm sorry you're finding out this way, but this is my husband, Owen."

# Chapter 9

## Owen

As the room around us buzzed, Emmeline's dad gave us both a look that couldn't be ignored. "Follow me, please." He placed a hand on his wife's back and guided the four of us through an exit I hadn't known was nearby. We traveled through the hotel's hallway, then to the elevators.

I felt like I was being called to the principal's office.

It wasn't until the doors closed that the sound of people calling mine and Emmeline's names were drowned out entirely.

"Mom—" she began but was interrupted by her dad.

"Let's wait until we're in the room."

The interior of the elevator seemed to increase in atmospheric pressure.

None of us spoke.

The silence was drawn-out and deafening.

I occupied one back corner and Emmeline leaned against the railing next to me. In the metal door's reflection, I discreetly watched Mrs. McCarthy's slow confused blinks. Following the line of her eyes, I realized they were focused on Em's hand gripping mine.

I assumed we were going somewhere quiet to talk, that her dad was probably not taking me to a higher floor to push me out a window, which might be preferable to the conversation we were about to have.

At least whatever came next would be private. I wondered if Emmeline would tell her parents the truth. Would that be the best way to go forward?

Stopping on the third floor, the doors opened. It wasn't a long walk before Mr. McCarthy slide a plastic key in the reader and held open the door for the rest of us to walk through. There was makeup and a curling iron on the vanity in the bathroom and an overnight bag was open on top of the dresser, but otherwise, it looked like any other hotel room. One king-sized bed with a floral print comforter and a mockingly serene painting of a beach on the wall.

"Em, what's going on?" he asked from behind us.

I tried to convey to Emmeline that she could tell them the truth, but instead, she said, "I'm married. This is my husband, Owen."

"How?" Her mom drew the word out, creating syllables that weren't there.

"We eloped."

"When?"

Emmeline half-looked, half-cringed at me.

I needed to line our stories up.

Taking a deep breath, I braced myself to lie to their faces. "I was in Arizona visiting a friend a while ago, and I kinda joked that she should meet me in Las Vegas." I shook my head at the feeble explanation. These people were going to hate me. "And she did."

Mrs. McCarthy continued blinking with her mouth hanging open. "We didn't even know you were dating anyone."

Mr. McCarthy crossed his arms over his broad chest. "You got married as a joke?"

"No." Emmeline's reply was firm. This time when she looked at me, it was with a tenderness that swelled in my chest. "I love him." Her conviction in those words would have convinced me if I didn't know otherwise.

But I did know. This wasn't real, and I needed to remember that. This would end in a fake divorce or blow up in our faces; there was no in between.

I wasn't even the guy she wanted at this party.

"Do you love her?" Mr. McCarthy bore holes into me with the force of his scrutiny.

"I do," I answered.

"Then why the hell with the secrecy?"

"I didn't know how you'd respond. It was sudden and kinda… rash," she explained.

Her mom scoffed, "You think?"

Mr. McCarthy narrowed his eyes at me. "Who are you?"

I buried my hands in my pockets and forced my shoulders down from my ears straightening my back. "I'm Owen Kauahi. I'm a veterinarian at a dog shelter."

"Oh…" Dawning lit Mrs. McCarthy's face before she looked at her husband. "The running buddy."

He shook his head, not comprehending.

Em nodded, her eyes regaining some of their brightness. "Exactly."

"I knew you liked him," her mom went on, the tension in her forehead softening.

A blush rose on Em's cheeks, and she glanced at me out of the corner of her eye.

"We just found out with everyone else." Her mom gestured vaguely at the floor, indicating where the party was still going on below us. "I just… I would have…" She sighed. "I would have liked to be at your wedding. I would have liked to know you were *dating* someone, let alone got *married*."

Mr. McCarthy nodded.

"I know." Emmeline crossed her arms over her chest. She was wrapped as tightly around herself as she could be. Seeing her like that made something in my chest constrict. Hooking my arm around her waist, I pulled her against my side, and she leaned into me.

Emmeline blinked at the ceiling, her eyes shining and wet. Her dad continued to glare at me, but I was more concerned about her. This was going to be a wedge in their relationship.

If my parents found out... My blood ran cold. My parents *couldn't* find out.

As if he could read my thoughts, Mr. McCarthy asked, "Do your parents know?"

I met his eye and shook my head. I felt like a teen who got caught sneaking into his daughter's room. But being the rule-abiding kid I was, I never had that experience, and I definitely didn't like this one.

He was a stranger, but his clear disappointment made me feel disgusted with myself.

"What's your name?" Mrs. McCarthy cut in, her words wobbled.

"Owen Kau—"

"Not you." She turned to her daughter. "You. What is your name?"

When Em only looked as confused as I felt, her mom groaned. "Did you take his name, Emmeline?"

"No."

"Why not?"

"I... It didn't seem necessary."

"Apparently, neither was telling your parents. Well, at least I've always known your legal name, then. There's that, at least."

It was clear I was the last person she wanted to hear speak, but I hoped I could find the right words. "I'm sorry. This is..."

Em's fingers tucked under her arm and entwined with mine.

The right words weren't there, or any words... "I hope you can forgive us someday."

Actually, I hoped they'd forgive Em; they could hate me for the rest of their lives, as long as they forgave her.

Mr. McCarthy scrubbed his palm over his jaw. "It's probably best that you two go."

"I am sorry you found out this way," Em said. I could hear the tight knot in her throat, strangling her. She clung to my hand like it was giving her strength.

"I'm sure you are." He wrapped his wife in his arms, who hid her face in his chest.

I had never felt so rotten in my life.

"We're gonna go..." Em said to the floor.

"I think that's best."

We stepped into the hall and waited for the elevator to arrive. In the reflection of the metal doors, Emmeline wiped her ring finger under her eyes.

"You okay?" I asked lamely.

Fanning her face, she blinked and took a deep breath. "It'll be fine."

"Want me to take you home?"

"We can't. We need to... I don't know, celebrate?" It was clear in her deflated tone that it was as appealing to her as it was to me.

The elevator dinged and the doors opened to an empty car. We stepped in and she pushed the button for the main floor.

"Would it be that bad to just disappear tonight?"

"Half of my clients and coworkers are here. We need to convince them." She leaned her head back against the wall, her eyes closed. "If we don't, then breaking my parents' hearts was for nothing." There was that tight sound in her voice again. She sniffled and shook her head, her curls shifting around her shoulders.

I hesitated to ask, but then curiosity won out. "Why didn't you tell them the truth?"

"I didn't want to tell Dad the reason. I don't know… It's stupid, but that man saying he wouldn't work with me was, like, humiliating. You know?"

I nodded.

She looked at me, her head still pressed against the elevator. "Thanks though. That was not fun back there."

My hand tingled to hold hers, but I kept it tucked in my pocket. "We'll get through this, Em."

We rode the rest of the way in silence. When we reached the bottom, the doors opened to the party waiting for us, loud and overwhelming. She squared her shoulders and took a step forward. I wasn't ready to follow her, not with my stomach in knots as it was. I wrapped a hand around her waist and pulled her back into the elevator car with me.

"What are you doing?" she asked, her back against my chest.

I pushed the close door button and then the five—the highest level the building had to offer. "You know, I've heard there's an amazing view of the Breslin Center here." I hoped my dry tone conveyed my joke.

Her reflection blinked in confusion.

"It'd be a shame to miss it."

"A view of the Breslin Center?" She looked over her shoulder at me. "Like where the Spartan basketball games happen?"

I nodded. My arm banded around her waist was loose, and if she moved forward, I'd let my arm drop.

She shook her head. "Are you avoiding going back to the party?"

"Of course not." I pretended to be appalled and was rewarded with a smile tugging on her lips. "I'm just a Breslin Center enthusiast."

That did it. A beautiful smile found a home on her lovely mouth—so close to mine. "I've never heard of such a thing."

"Oh yeah, we enthusiasts are everywhere."

The doors opened to an empty hall, just like the one her parents' room was on. Without any excuse to stay in the position we had been in, my arm fell back to my side and she stepped away from me.

There were faint sounds from inside the rooms as we stepped onto the swirl-patterned carpet. Our strides lined up, the backs of our hands brushing every once in a while. She kept casting me amused glances out of the corner of her eye.

A lone window sat at the end of the hall, and we stopped in front of it. Soft snow fell from the black sky, the flakes catching the light from the lampposts in the parking lot below. At the intersection, the traffic light changed from red to green, and just beyond that, through bare trees lining the river, was the Breslin Center. The LED sign on the corner read "Happy New Year!" then switched to an image of a Spartan player dunking a basketball.

It was just a circular building, with a brick exterior, surrounded by parking lots and snow-covered grass. But I held my hands out dramatically. "I mean," with wide eyes, I looked at Emmeline as I breathed, "wow."

"That is the Breslin Center..." She laughed, though it lacked her normal freedom as if her joy was tethered.

I couldn't blame her.

"It sure is."

"And you're an enthusiast... of the Breslin Center? Not basketball?"

"What's that?"

"You're ridiculous."

I grinned back at her. The cold seeped from outside through the window into my sweater. Judging by her hand running down the sleeve of her dress, she felt it, too.

"You ready to celebrate this momentous sight?" I jerked my head back the way we had come, just in time for the second elevator doors to open and two people spilled out. Their mouths were interlocked, and his hands were on her ass as she pulled at his belt. They did not notice Emmeline or me as he pressed a key card to open a door and fell into it.

Em's cheeks were red, and her eyes widened when she looked back at me.

I shrugged. "That's the power of the Breslin Center, baby."

She barked a laugh, one that sounded closer to her normal one. "I get it now."

I nodded smugly. "I knew you would."

The elevator ride down to the main floor was less weighted this time, the sound of the party less daunting.

Just outside the opened door, Emmeline took my hand. "Owen, how many drinks does it take to get you to dance?"

I narrowed my eyes at her.

"Could it happen before midnight?"

With our fingers still entwined, I tilted her wrist. It was a quarter to eleven. A lot had happened in the past forty-five minutes.

"Not likely."

She gave me a deviant eyebrow raise and tugged me directly to the bar.

***

Emmeline was very efficient when she set her mind to a task. Her ability to sense a near-empty drink was otherworldly. We'd started with a shot, then she'd pulled out the big dogs with a couple of Long Island iced teas.

It was eleven-fifty, and I was sweating on the dance floor.

I resisted as long as I could. But little by little, my head bobbing to the beat led to my shoulders joining in until there wasn't any reason to remain at the tall table we occupied with her brother and brother-in-law.

Someone else must have gained control of the music because it had shifted from 90s country to early 2000s hip-hop. There was probably a joke in there about the music being from this decade in an hour or so, but I was too drunk to find it.

Too drunk and too consumed with Emmeline.

I'd taken my sweater off and rolled up the sleeves of my button-up. Emmeline watched the process with a hunger I would have thought I'd imagined, if her hands didn't run along the cords of my forearms repeatedly. The brush of her fingertips on my skin sent shivers through my scalp.

Sweat mixed with her coconut scent, warm and enticing. She swayed with me, her perfect fucking hip under my hand and her firm thighs against mine. If I pressed in any direction, she followed my lead. She took when I gave with barely a breath between our bodies.

Songs blended together. We changed positions—chest to chest, her back to my front. I was even feeling loose enough to spin and dip her during a slow song. She threw her head back and laughed—her hair grazing the floor, her throat exposed. I barely refrained from gliding my lips from under her jaw to her clavicle.

That intoxicating hunger was back in her eyes. "You're really good at this."

"You are, too." I cupped my palm against hers by our shoulders.

"Are you having fun?"

I nodded. "You?"

"I am, but I'm a little disappointed you aren't wearing the 'arm candy' attire you had promised."

My fingers flexed on her side. "Disappointed? I'm showing my forearms for you."

Her eyes dropped to my mouth, possibly because I already watched hers. Her white teeth bit into the full flesh of her lower lip as her mouth curved into a smile. "Oh, I noticed."

It was a struggle to keep my breathing normal, but if I breathed the way my body needed, I'd be inhaling like we'd just finished a run. Instead, I brought in just enough oxygen to avoid getting lightheaded.

"I would offer to switch outfits, but I like this dress on you," I said.

Her petite breasts pressed against the deep V of her neckline. At this close proximity, there was no way she didn't notice me looking. "Thank you. I feel pretty hot in it."

The alcohol was clearly affecting my inhibitions because I met her eyes with heated intent. "You are hot, Emmeline," I murmured, my voice pitched low.

The black pupils surrounded by blue-green irises widened and fixed again on my mouth. "Too bad you usually catch me all sweaty and messy after our runs."

I splayed my hands across her back, pressing her stomach to mine. "I like that, too."

Our mouths were so close, I couldn't see hers anymore—just her eyes searching mine. My heart thundered against my ribs—a persistent demand for more of her. More contact, more of whatever she was going to say next. More of whatever it was that was growing between us.

"I like—"

Her uncle's voice came over the speakers, cutting off whatever she was going to say. She had to look over her shoulder to see him. The slender blonde who'd introduced herself to me as Aunt Lucy was tucked in the crook under Mr. Mayn-Mr. McCarthy's—arm. "Alright, everyone, five minutes to midnight! Find your sweetheart!" He looked down at the woman at his side with a sly smile.

There was a commotion around us. I straightened and my arms fell from around Emmeline, but she didn't step back. Her hands slid up my forearms and gripped just under my cuffed sleeves.

The line of what we did for show and what we did because we wanted to was skewed. Even with that, it was obvious we were attracted to each other. Apparently, the chemistry I felt for her wasn't as one-sided as I'd thought. But there was still the question of if it was just attraction or something more.

It was definitely something more for me.

*Way more.*

"Toast?" A waiter stood at my side, his tray filled with champagne flutes.

"Yes, thank you." I took one for myself and handed another to Em. "Should we go back to the table with your brother?"

"Um..." She pressed tight to my side and whispered in my ear, "We have more eyes on us here. Is it okay if we do the kiss here?"

My body went cold. "Sure."

Taking a sip, I tried to hide my disappointment. It was all a show—a couple of drinks, a couple of minutes of dancing, a few flirtatious looks and comments...

And I'd fallen for it.

"Thirty seconds everyone," Mr. McCarthy's omniscient voice directed.

Her head rested on my shoulder. "I may be more drunk than I realized. Everything is starting to spin."

I wrapped my arm around her waist. "Do you need to sit down?"

Her hair tickled my chin as she nuzzled closer. "I'm okay."

*Someone must be watching.* I didn't look around to see for sure, since it wouldn't help her display if they could see the pain I felt.

The countdown started around us. We joined in, each number grew louder as we neared the end of this year and the beginning of the next.

"One!" we yelled.

Her arms went into the air and then wrapped around my shoulders, the base of her glass pressed against my back. My arms hooked around the small of her back, and I pulled her to me. She tilted her head and her lips brushed mine.

Electricity sparked behind my closed eyelids.

I pulled her tighter as my free hand traveled up her back to cup her damp neck under her hair. Her abs flexed, and I felt more than heard her moan against my mouth.

Gently. Savoring, I sucked her pouty lower lip between my teeth. My body was lit with sensations—the taste of her, the smell of her, the feel of her. I drew her closer, finding every millimeter of space between us and closing it. Her fingers squeezed my deltoid, and the pressure of her nails over my shirt made me wish we were alone. That this kiss wasn't for the benefit of our lie.

Her ribs expanded against my arm when I slipped my teeth from her delicious mouth.

Her eyes opened slow and heavy, her lips slightly parted—the picture of a woman consumed by the effects of a good kiss.

If it was a show, it was a good one.

# Chapter 10

## Emmeline

Dreams of a party full of people simultaneously laughing and throwing sneers my way faded as I woke. My drowsy, aching head recognized that I was in Owen's bed, but not much else.

We'd stumbled through his front door around two AM, with the headlights of Malcolm's car stretching our shadows across the living room floor. I waved through the open door, the final assurance to my brother that he and Tom could head home. The door closed, leaving us surrounded by Owen's darkened house. The sound of dogs barking came from down the hall and straight ahead of me. A large, long-haired St. Bernard woofed half-heartedly from the sofa, while an angry chihuahua tried to climb the baby-gate separating it from me. I got Owen and myself a glass of water from his little kitchen while he disappeared to let three dogs loose from wherever they'd been held.

In his absence, I gave the little dog plenty of space. It was a whirlwind meeting the other members of the pack. I had been drunk and dizzy, and the dogs were excited and sweet. I couldn't stop laughing at their antics to squeeze up to me.

Once I had looked up and found Owen watching me like he didn't quite know me, but the expression cleared as he nodded toward the hall. I followed him—my feet and legs happy to stretch after a night in heels, even if his hardwood floors were cold.

His stride had a little more sway in the shoulders than normal, but it still held his confident athleticism. That rhythmic shift of his body that I liked so much. The way his muscles flexed as he ran. The way his shoes hit the concrete with a metronome-like consistency.

"Here's the thing…" he began. "I don't have a spare room. The sofa isn't really an option because Maui and Ella sleep there. Ella has pretty bad arthritis, and I don't have the heart to make her sleep anywhere else."

We entered the bedroom at the end of the hall. It was filled with a gigantic bed. And just like that, my mind immediately went to thoughts of how to use up all that space.

"It's a big bed, but if you'd rather not share, I can make up a bed on the floor. I'll be fine there—"

"No," I interrupted. "No, it's totally fine. I'm sure you'll find a way to resist me."

He chuckled, but it didn't sound quite right—there was a raw edge to it. Nodding, he turned his back to me and pulled open a couple of drawers. A few moments later, the drawers were closed, and he held something out to me.

I took it without thinking, soft cotton cradled in my hands. "What's this?"

"For you to sleep in."

"Oh, I hadn't thought that far ahead."

The bed grew even larger, taking up more space in the room.

There were moments throughout the night that felt *real*. The way he danced and looked at me. The way his kiss made my toes curl. But there was an invisible line down the center of the bed that neither of us crossed.

I would not consider last night's sleep restful. Even in our inebriated states, we never crossed the invisible centerline of the bed. I fell asleep disappointed and aching.

My eyes were still closed, fused shut from the mascara I hadn't removed the night before, as I slowly became aware of warm breath on my neck. Then, the press of a warm body to my back. There was the faint smell of wintergreen on the sheets and something else—something that was not good, but not unpleasant, either.

There was a heavy pain at the base of my skull that would only grow if I didn't get water and food in me quickly. But still, I snuggled back against the chest rising and falling behind me.

It scooted closer, and the breathing changed to sniffing. Quick bursts of inhalations edged closer to my face and four bony paws padded my back.

Groaning and laughing, I pressed my face into the pillow for protection. The dog shifted for more reach, a cold nose against my ear. The bed swayed with the momentum of its wagging tail.

This was not great for my hangover.

"Venice, come on, girl. Let Em be." I heard Owen's voice somewhere by his bedroom door over the dog's excited whimpers. Its wet nose stamped my neck and cheek. I pressed my face deeper into the pillow, hoping he wouldn't see the makeup mess I was sure was there.

A second dog's weight depressed the bed on the side Owen no longer slept on. Venice stopped her assault to focus on the newcomer. I grunted as her back paws landed by my spine.

"Bandit, Venice," Owen's command halted the playful growls, "down."

One of the dogs made a sound of protest while the other's claws clicked on the floor as it jumped off the bed.

"Bandit, down," he repeated more forcefully. This time, the dog obeyed. There were sounds of claws scuttling and then the click of the bedroom door closing. I peeked out from the pillow, but when I saw him standing at the edge of the bed, I hid my face again.

"Sorry about that."

"It's okay."

"Here's some water and ibuprofen."

"Thank you. Can you put it on the bedside table?"

"Is it too bright in here? I could—"

"No." Blinds and curtains were drawn over the morning sunlight, making the room gloriously dark.

There was a pause before he said, "Okay, uh... there's some sweats, T-shirt, and a towel in the bathroom when you're ready to get up. There's coffee brewed, so help yourself to anything in the kitchen. I'll keep the door closed so the dogs don't bother you again. Sleep as long as you want. I'll be back in thirty minutes or so."

"Where are you going?"

"To take Bandit for a bike ride."

"Aren't you hungover?" I rolled onto my side in outrage, my make-up-smeared appearance be damned. How dare he feel well enough to exercise while I was trying to build up the tolerance to trudge to the bathroom.

His eyebrows shot up and his eyes widened at the sight of me. I must look shocking or frightening; at least, that's what his expression said. He looked... devastating. So beautiful in his dark gray jacket, zipped up to his scruffy chin. He wore a stocking cap pulled down over his ears and his cheekbones were high and sharp.

"Ugh," I groaned. "You feel fine, don't you?"

He chuckled and hung his head. "No, I showered, drank water, then coffee, ate toast, and showered again. But if I don't take Bandit for at least a mile jog, he is intolerable the entire day." Helplessly, Owen shrugged. "High-energy dog. But if it makes you feel any better, I might puke when I get back."

"Do not talk about puking."

"Right, sorry."

Growling and barking erupted on the other side of the closed door.

"Christ." Owen set the glass of water and pill bottle on his bedside table. "I gotta get Bandit out of this house before Maui kills him."

"Is that the grumpy little dog?"

"Yeah."

"Okay, so..." I counted the names off on my fingers. "Ella, Venice, Bandit, Maui, and..."

"Indie. She won't have much to do with you until she gets to know you. If you venture out into the living room, just don't go near Maui. He's an asshole."

It hurt my face to smile, so it was short-lived there. "We all have our moments."

"Yeah, well, Maui only has moments."

"I'll give him space." I pushed up into a sitting position in the middle of the bed. I rubbed my hands over my face, then reached toward the ceiling in a stretch. My back arched and my eyes closed, releasing some of the tightness in my shoulders.

When I opened my eyes, Owen's head was tilted, the tip of his tongue trapped between his teeth. His eyes slowly traveled up my neck to my eyes. There was the same heat there I'd seen the night before. Over the rim of a glass as he took a drink or when his hand held my waist while we moved together to the music pounding through the speakers. I was dancing in victory then, but in my current state, I wasn't sure if my goal had been worth it. It had taken a lot of alcohol to get him on the dance floor, and now I was paying the price.

Then, of course, there was when the party around us counted from ten to Happy New Year. All I could see was his face—his lips softly parted, his eyes focused on me. He didn't count down; his eyes remained trained on me, full of anticipation from behind an unseen boundary. Paused in limbo, not in heaven, nowhere near hell.

Then that one kiss... Everything stilled except for the drum of my heart.

A brush of lips, the gentle scrape of teeth, the glide of his tongue just inside of my mouth.

A shiver raced down my spine.

I wanted to do it again.

I'd assumed the heated looks were for the benefit of watching eyes, but there was no one watching now.

My chest grazed against the cotton of the T-shirt I'd borrowed the night before. The soft material did nothing to hide my bra-less state.

A muscle jumped in his jaw as he swallowed, his eyes falling briefly before landing back on mine. Whatever thoughts were playing behind those hazel depths only inspired my imagination.

Something fell in the living room with a loud thud, startling us out of our unexpected staring contest.

"Fuck," he said to the closed door. "I'm gonna... I'll be back. Just, ya know... make yourself at home or whatever."

"Um... Thanks."

The latch clicked shut behind him, leaving me alone in his room. I let my face fall into my hands. I was too hungover and tired for the tension that had just soared between us. Everything we were up against was too much of a mess to add mutual attraction. But it was there.

And my body still thrummed from it.

Need pulsed between my legs in time with the quick pace of my heart.

Sighing, I dropped my hands to the back of my neck and rubbed. I had to stretch to reach the provisions he'd left for me. I downed the water and medication in hopes they'd make living a bit more bearable. With clumsy movements, I picked up my cell and called Laurie. I intended to leave a voicemail—assuming she'd still be sleeping—but surprisingly, she picked up on the second ring.

"What the hell is going on?" she answered in a scratchy voice, foregoing a polite greeting. "My dad left me some bizarre message at like, two in the morning." It sounded like she was just as miserable as I was.

"Laurie, I fucked up."

"Okay, so you *did* announce your elopement last night?"

"Yeah..."

In the silence that followed, I relived the terrible scene with my parents and the disappointment on their faces.

"Pretty chill night then, huh?" Laurie croaked.

I snorted. "Absolutely nothing of note. Glad to know your dad is sharing the happy news."

"You know how subtle he is. So... I think I know what your husband looks like. I think he's the latest man my dad was trying to convince to date me. Smokin' hot, crazy sexy mouth, veterinarian."

"That's Owen."

"Congratulations."

"You're being very calm about all this."

"I don't have the energy to be appalled right now. Give me, like, a gallon of water and twenty-four hours."

"How was your night?"

"I'm still single, so according to my dad, a total failure."

I chuckled. "Don't make laugh, it hurts."

"So, what's your plan?"

"I don't know. We haven't talked about it yet, but probably an amicable divorce in a couple of weeks. I'll get my client switched to someone else and... probably avoid the shame of all this by moving to Anchorage or something."

"Solid." I heard her open the cupboards in her kitchen. "Ugh. I need coffee, but that would require grinding beans."

"Oh right. Owen made coffee."

"You really should reconsider that divorce, Em."

"I thought I told you not to make me laugh," I groaned and inch-wormed toward the edge of the bed.

"No seriously, what's wrong with this guy?"

"Nothing that I can tell."

"Then why aren't you into him?"

"Laur, that's the problem. I *am* into him." My heart gave a sad little twist. "He's not into me. Or... I don't know. Either way, pretending to be married seems like a sure way to implode any potential for a real relationship."

"That's probably true. How am I supposed to talk to my parents about this?"

"Malcolm said he knew. I don't want to make you lie, but just please don't tell them the truth. Sorry to put you in this position."

"Aw, Em, this sucks. I know you don't generally jive with lying. Don't worry about me. I'll find a way to talk to them that I'm cool with."

"Good."

Opening the door to the hallway, I could hear a grumpy harrumph from one of the dogs in the living room, but that was it. The welcoming and comforting smell of coffee guided me to the kitchen. From behind the baby-gate separating the kitchen and the living room, Venice tilted her head in a silent beg for attention.

"I'll be right there. I just need to not be so miserable first." I opened and closed a cupboard in search of a coffee mug.

"Who are you talking to?" Laurie asked.

"One of his dogs."

"Oh, he has dogs? That's cute."

"He actually has five."

"What?" She drew out the word, as if winding up.

"Yeah, they were all..." I paused in my explanation.

I'd found the mugs but was distracted by a white board hanging inside the door. It listed each dogs' name and medications, as well as food, activity, and vet visit schedules. The full scope of Owen's commitment splayed out in graph form. He'd taken these dogs on, each a special case in one way or another. The most confusing was Venice. Next to her name there was a list of items—sock, remote, candle, half a loaf of bread. The words seemed random, but there was no way that was true.

"They were all what?" Laurie jogged me back to the present.

"Uh, dogs at his work. They weren't getting adopted, so he took them in."

"Is he gonna get more?"

I scanned over the white board again. "I hope not."

I took a deep whiff of coffee before sipping it. The ceramic cup clunked onto the counter-top as I rubbed my forehead. "I'm gonna take a shower."

"You're drinking coffee right now, aren't you?" Through the phone pressed between my ear and shoulder, I could hear her resentment.

"No...?"

"You're going to have to work on that lying if you're gonna pull this off."

# CHAPTER 11

## OWEN

Even wearing his weighted vest, Bandit pulled me and the bike for the whole three-mile ride. I did my best, but I felt like trash. We barely finished our usual twenty-minute route in thirty-five minutes, and that was still faster than I would have gone without his pressure. But hell, I wouldn't have left the house without his pressure.

I wouldn't have left my bed.

My bed where I had left Emmeline.

Why did I have so many goddamn dogs?

Not that she'd want me in bed with her. It was a disappointing truth, but it was true.

Bandit's tongue hung out of his mouth as he waited for me to punch in the code to the garage door opener. Hanging his vest next to his lead took far more energy than it usually did—energy I did not have.

I opened the door to the dining area. A cacophony of barking erupted from the living room and was returned by Bandit. They beat like a drum set played without rhythm—reverberating through my cranium.

Opening the gate, I let Bandit join his pack. Venice and Indie began playing with him, while Maui barked at the side of the sofa. I ran my fingers through the soft hair atop Ella's head, and her tail padded on the cushion. Her arthritis seemed to have flared. I'd have to do X-rays this week and maybe switch up her physical therapy.

The door to the bathroom opened, and Emmeline emerged with a towel wrapped around her hair. I'd given her a work fundraiser T-shirt from a couple of years ago. I was only slightly larger than her, so the shirt was a pretty good fit. My black sweatpants were cinched around her hips, the white strings tied in a droopy bow. She looked at me with a makeup-free face, her eyes no longer surrounded by the dark charcoal that had been there this morning. She'd looked up at me from my pillow, her eyelids heavy, and I'd leaned away from the startling force of her eyes. But even clean, they were just as striking. Long, pale lashes against pink skin. Her complexion was even ruddier than normal.

"Hot shower?" I asked.

"Did you expect me to take a cold one?"

"Nah, it's just you're really red."

*Smooth, dude. No wonder she can't resist you.*

"Right." She sighed. "Just one of the perks of being translucent."

"No, I didn't... It's not... bad." I crossed my arms over my chest and I kinda wished I could disappear. When did I get this awkward?

"I know. I was just joking." She chewed on her bottom lip.

I searched my brain for anything to talk about, but instead, I conjured up an image of her in my shower. The shifting shades of her naked skin, her hands lathering soap over her calves and thighs. Her hair a wet mass between her shoulder blades. My hands discovering a path from her hips, up her stomach, to cup her breasts.

"Mal texted."

I was uncomfortably jarred out of my thoughts.

"He and Tom are going to drop my car off this evening, and then we can get your car," she said after a few beats.

"Cool." I nodded to the floor, thankful she couldn't read my mind.

"How was the bike ride?"

I smirked and rolled my eyes. "Miserable."

"It's sweet that you did it anyway, though."

"Ugh, not really. It was self-preservation. I'm not going to do much of anything for the rest of the day."

"You're right, it wasn't sweet at all. It was a totally selfish act."

"That's right." I smirked.

"Your coffee is good."

"Thank you." I nodded to the open door behind her. "I'm gonna take a third shower this morning."

She cringed, her shoulders lifting toward her ears. "There isn't any hot water left."

Considering what the thought of her wet and hot was doing to my body, a cold shower would probably be beneficial.

I emerged from the bathroom after a frigid, quick wash off, yet my blood still simmered for Emmeline. A craving still absent from my tongue, my hands still regretfully empty.

I found her in the kitchen, scraping scrambled eggs onto two plates. She looked over her shoulder and gave me a closed-mouth smile. I shrugged; my T-shirt felt too tight in the shoulders and around the chest. It had more to do with how tightly wound I was and less about the fit.

"You made breakfast?"

The toaster popped two slices of toast.

"I needed some protein," she responded, reaching around me to grab the hot bread.

We didn't touch.

It was too much not to touch her.

Placing my hands on each of her shoulders, I looked directly into her eyes. "This makes you my best friend."

Her hair smelled like my shampoo. I missed the coconut scent, but I liked smelling me on her, even if it was just from a bottle in my shower.

She chuckled. "I thought Remi was your best friend."

"Fuck Remi," I joked.

"Oh my god! Poor Remi."

"He's fine. Under the circumstances, he'd sell me out for scrambled eggs, too."

Her smile killed me a thousand beautiful ways, every single time.

"I thought you were more loyal than that."

I shook my head. "Loyalty to my wife will always come first."

Her eyebrow quirked. "Even your fake wife?"

"Yeah." I smiled back at her while putting more distance between us. It was a good reminder that this was a temporary episode. A break from our regularly scheduled lives, even if seeing her wake up in my bed and wearing my clothes was even better than I'd imagined.

Even if everything in me wanted everything in her.

"Speaking of... we should figure out," she gestured to the space between us, "what this is."

I turned to pour myself another cup of coffee and hid any eagerness I felt. "What this is?"

"Like... how long is this arrangement gonna go on for?"

Swallowing, I nodded. "Um, I was thinking a couple of weeks... middle of January sort of thing? But far enough from Valentine's that it's not on anyone's mind. Do you want anything to drink?"

She carried our plates to the table and sat.

"I'm good," she said, holding up her mug as proof. "Okay, so a couple of weeks. Do we just live together or... I never really thought about what makes people seem married."

I sat across from her; the table was small enough that our knees brushed. Resting my forehead on my fist, I picked up my toast and took a buttery bite. "They do things together, right? So, I don't know, I have an open house for work next weekend… Can you come to that?"

"Sure."

She stared into space for a moment. "So… why do we get divorced? I don't want it to be either of our faults, and I want to be friends after of this, ya know?"

*Friends.* I'd decided months ago that if that was all we were, then it was enough.

I nodded and took another bite. "I haven't figured that out yet. Can we figure it out later?"

"Okay." She rolled her neck from shoulder to shoulder.

"You okay?" I asked before sipping my coffee.

"Just sore. My neck and shoulders."

"Do you want some wintergreen oil?"

She blinked, her eyebrows drawn together.

I shrugged. "It's good for sore muscles."

"Is that why you always smell delicious?"

"Delicious?"

"Yeah, like something that would taste really good."

"I know the definition of delicious, Em."

She rolled her eyes.

"I use it pretty much every day. It's actually a massage oil with lots of wintergreen in it."

Her pale eyebrow lifted. "A massage, you say?"

"You want me to give you one?" My heart rate picked up.

"Would you? I don't want to make things weirder."

"I don't know how things could get any weirder."

She licked her lips and looked down at her plate.

Resting my elbows on the tabletop, I pressed my lips to my clasped hands. Neither of us said anything, but we both knew it *could* get weirder. Sex had a habit of complicating things.

I leaned back in my chair. "I think a massage will be fine."

She smiled at me. "Then a massage would be great."

"Give me some time for my head to not hurt?"

She rolled her eyes sarcastically. "Fine."

"Are you still hungry?" I pointed to her empty plate.

She shook her head.

"I'll get the dishes done."

She sat at the kitchen table while I rinsed and loaded the dishes. Venice kept her company, rubbing her nose under Em's hand to beg for more petting.

More than once we caught each other looking. I loved the feel of her eyes on me. Normally, any kind of attention made me itch, but not when it came to Emmeline.

Closing the dishwasher, I leaned a hip against the counter. "Wanna watch some TV or something?"

"Sure." She stroked Venice one more time before standing. At the entrance to the living room, she paused. "Where are we sitting?"

The sofa, as usual, was taken up by Maui and Ella, leaving only the recliner that I usually lounged in.

"You take the chair, I'll get set up on the floor."

I snapped my fingers, and after some convincing, I got all the dogs outside to do their business. Once I sat down, I didn't want to get up for a while.

From the closet next to the bathroom, I grabbed a couple of blankets and pillows. Em sat in the recliner with her feet curled under her.

"Blanket?" I held my favorite quilt out to her—it was one my grandma sewed when I was a kid. The fabric was extra soft after thousands of washes, and the pink, teal, and purple colors had long since faded.

Emmeline took it and tucked it around herself. "Thank you."

I nodded and swallowed back the strange surge of sentimentality the sight made me feel.

It was ten more minutes before I had the dogs settled with toys filled with frozen peanut butter to distract them. I laid on the floor with a pillow under my head and the cushiest blanket I had underneath me. We settled on a murder mystery that she'd mentioned wanting to watch a few weeks ago.

The movie was good, but it wasn't enough to earn one hundred percent of my attention. If I was being honest, it hardly kept twenty percent.

Em was a jumpy viewer, and she did this cute gasp thing at the big reveal. She traced her fingers over the stitching, tracking a star shape out of the triangles sewn together.

The credits were rolling when she asked, "Can we talk about the fact that you danced with me last night? Or is part of your no-dancing rule... that it can never be spoken of?"

"Can we talk about how we're both paying for that today?" I rolled from my side onto my back. My ankles were crossed by the base of her chair.

"Okay, but you're not a bad dancer. Like, you're pretty good."

I shrugged. I felt a familiar twist of my stomach, wondering if people had watched me. "Being good isn't the problem."

"Then what is?"

"It's probably a holdover from middle school dances when kids would ask me to teach them the hula."

Her eyebrows shot up. "Oh no."

"Yeah, it was awkward. *Lilo and Stitch* had just come out and the part where it was culturally significant just flew over their heads."

Cringing she said, "I would like to think that I wouldn't have done that to you when I was a kid, but I one hundred percent would have."

"I would like to think the kids that did it have grown into adults who wouldn't, and maybe they're even raising kids that wouldn't..."

"Hopefully."

"I also don't like attention."

"Hmm. Then last night really sucked. Why not?"

"Nothing major, I just don't. Shy, I guess."

She looked down and watched her fingers as they traced the seams. "Then can we talk about the kiss?"

I was hyperaware of every breath that lifted my chest. The thump of my heart against my ribs. The way her hand had frozen in its nervous progress. And the way she licked her lips.

Even through the fog of alcohol and my hangover, that one kiss was sketched in vivid detail in my mind. But I thought it was for the benefit of other people.

"What about it?" I asked, my voice surprisingly normal. "I thought it was pretty convincing."

Running her fingers through her hair, she blocked my view of her face. "Oh yeah... it was probably convincing."

We startled at the knock on the door, followed by the raucous barking of five dogs.

# Chapter 12

## Emmeline

"Do you need more space?" Owen asked, standing behind me at the entrance of his bedroom closet.

"I can make do," I answered.

I had returned almost two hours prior, after dropping Owen off at his car and getting a few provisions from my house. Malcolm and Tom knocking on the door when they did probably saved me from some embarrassment. But despite the flames licking through my veins as Owen stared up at me or that the kiss had felt *very* real, it was all in my head.

The rest of the evening fell into the safe normal pattern we always found. We joked and laughed, and everything was completely normal. And I did not bring up the kiss again. I tried to not even think about it, but that was difficult to do.

It was like a bruise I kept forgetting was there, only then I'd touch it again, bringing it back to the forefront of my mind.

"You sure you don't want more space?"

He'd cleared room in the closet for me while I was out.

Packing had been difficult. I brought the essentials and very little else. But the essentials list was pretty long for a couple weeks stay—clothes, beauty products, pillow, laptop, even some of my favorite foods. His eyebrow lift was the only indication that Owen was concerned about the suitcases and totes tucked into the back of my car and trunk.

"I have a recliner we can bring over. I didn't have room in my car, obviously," I offered.

"You're bringing a chair?"

"Don't you think I should?"

He shrugged. "I guess."

"I don't have to. Dibs on your chair forever then."

I should probably feel like I was taking up too much space and making myself too at home. But I didn't. I felt like I fit here with him.

There was that bruise again.

From behind my back, he snorted. "No, you're right... It's a good plan."

I shoved at a hanger, trying to inch more room out of the curtain rod.

"I'll box a couple more things up," he said, approaching my shoulder.

"You don't have to. I really can make do."

Instead of answering me, he plucked out a few shirts and pants. The fit would still be tight, but it was doable. It was nice of him. He was being very nice. But I was hyperaware of his proximity—how his strong hands gripped the hanger hooks and his bicep flexed against his sleeve. It was ridiculous to be turned-on by him moving clothes. Ridiculous.

"Thanks," I mumbled.

"Sure." He sounded completely unaffected. I guess it was only me who had a fetish for closet arrangement.

There was something about moving my things into his place that made this whole mess a little more... I don't know. It was already pretty serious and dramatic, so it wasn't that. But there was a finality in this. It was concrete in a way it hadn't been before.

I was pretending to have a husband. I was pretending to be a wife.

If anyone told me this was a lie they were living, I would think they were completely unhinged. There wasn't any part of this that was normal.

Yet, it didn't feel all that strange.

Maybe the strangeness would seep in later. There was no way we could cohabit so easily.

After brushing my teeth and washing my face, I stepped out of his bathroom into the bedroom. He sat against the headboard with a book in his lap. I could feel him not looking at me, or maybe I was just projecting how hard it was not to look at him.

His flannel sheets were soft against the skin exposed by my shorts. It wasn't my bed, but it felt really good to lay down. I was too drunk last night and too hungover this morning to appreciate how comfortable his mattress and bedding were. As he closed his book and laid flat, I rubbed my legs together. Somehow, in the shifting, I grazed against his calf.

We both went completely still.

We were so close.

It was all too off-putting and intense.

As if orchestrated, I rolled away from him at the same time he rolled away from me.

***

"I have to take Ella to my work. Do you wanna come?" Owen asked the next morning. "It won't be that long."

I looked up from my phone, pausing the mug of coffee pressed to my lips, it's fragrant contents warm and soothing. It wasn't as addicting as the sight of Owen fresh from the shower, with his white T-shirt clinging to his torso. Gray joggers hung low on his hips and cuffed at his ankles just above his bare feet. It felt risqué to see his toes.

And that was ridiculous.

Of course, his toes weren't risqué.

But I was definitely blushing.

"Uh… sure." I took a sip of my coffee, buying myself time to sound and act like a grown-ass woman. "What time are we leaving?"

"No big rush. Couple of hours?"

"Cool. Speaking of work, I forgot yesterday… I have a client appreciation dinner a week from Friday. Do you think we can keep this up until then?" I stood and walked to the living room. Passing Maui, he only growled at me a little. *Progress.*

"Sure."

"If you need a break from me or whatever, I can stay with Mal and Tom for a while."

He was silent for a beat. "Yeah, I mean, if you want to you can."

"I'm good." I cringed with my back to him. "Just you know… If you want me to, like if having me around gets… suffocating or whatever."

"Em."

I turned to face him.

"You're not suffocating. Have I made you think that you are?"

"No, it's just… I know you don't do relationships and you like your privacy; I just don't want to be too much. I feel like I'm really settling in, and I don't want you to feel like I'm over-staying my welcome."

I sat on the floor, facing him. I took one last drink before setting my coffee down in preparation to stretch. My body was still dehydrated from Thursday night, and my muscles were sore. I rolled my head to my shoulder and held it there, feeling the muscles give.

He sat in the recliner. "What do you mean, I don't do relationships?"

I crossed my arm over my chest. "Um... I thought you didn't."

"Why?"

"I've known you for a year, and I don't think you've ever gone on a date with anyone. The only time you've mentioned a girlfriend was from like, *years* ago, in vet school." Now that I said it out loud, I wondered if I'd made an assumption and then decided it was true.

"Huh. I'm not against relationships. Natalie, my ex... it wasn't always good, you know? And when we broke up, it hurt, so I don't want to date just anyone." I left out the part about how it had shaken my confidence. "If I'm going to try a relationship, I'd have to really trust that person."

"What do you mean, it wasn't always good?"

He ran a hand down his face, then cupped the back of his neck. "Uh... I never really knew what to think. You know, if she had a bad day, she'd take it out on me. That sort of thing."

I had an instant distaste for this woman.

"It's like we've taken the opposite approach to heartbreak," I said.

"Who broke your heart?"

"I don't have any one person; just different guys making little breaks, ya know?"

His brows pinched together, and he shook his head.

I filled my lungs and stretched my hands toward my feet. "One guy stood me up one too many times, so if a guy seems flakey, I cut it off. One guy cheated on me, so now if anyone seems too flirtatious with someone else, I cut it off."

"I didn't know that. It kinda surprises me." Quickly, he added, "Not that you'd have strong boundaries, but that…"

"I'd be cut-throat about it?"

"Kinda."

"I don't want to put my energy into a lost cause."

"You're right. Opposite approaches."

I sat up. He was looking at me, but his eyes were full of introspection.

"Do you ever wonder if… the self-protection has gone too far?" I asked.

He nodded.

"Me, too."

Just looking at him shouldn't fill me with so much need, but it did. I was nothing but need.

Need to look at him, need to look away.

Need to touch him, need to keep my hands to myself.

And this talk, this display of trust, only made it worse.

It would be good to go to his work and get out of the house. This energy between us needed to go somewhere else. It kept ricocheting off the walls. At night, it was trapped under the blankets, bouncing off the sheets like UV-rays in the atmosphere. I was going to get burned, though I didn't think I really cared.

Or maybe I cared too much.

# CHAPTER 13

## OWEN

*How's your "fake" wife doing?* Remi texted.

I glanced up from my screen to be sure Em couldn't see it. She sat with her legs spread in front of her, leaning her nose toward her knee in a stretch. It had me wishing I'd chosen to wear something other than gray sweatpants. I should have known better after last night since I woke up painfully needing release.

***Get rid of the quotation marks. This actually is fake,*** I typed.

***Yeah, sure it is.***

***Do you know how nuptials work?***

***It seems very convenient that the woman living in your house and sharing your bed just happens to be the one you will not shut up about.***

I was typing a reply one-handed of ***Bullshit,*** when he sent a second text. ***Well, your version of not shutting up.***

I checked again that she wasn't looking, even though there was no way she could see my screen from that angle. ***Look man, this is a very weird situation. She and I are not fucking.***

Unfortunately.

***It is fuckin' weird,*** he agreed.

I snorted.

Em looked over her shoulder as she twisted her spine in a stretch. "What's going on?"

We'd both fallen into ourselves after the talk we'd had about our past relationships. There was something there that I needed to figure out, some truth I hadn't realized about myself. But so far, it eluded me.

"Nothing, just talking to my friend," I answered.

"Remi from Arizona?"

"That's the one."

*The one at the origination of this whole mess.*

"How do you know him?"

"Vet school." My phone buzzed again, but I was too busy watching the way her leggings clung to her thighs like a second skin to check the notification. "Your back hurt?"

"I just feel really stiff."

"Is it my bed?"

"I think it's residual from the alcohol."

I licked my lips. It was a bad idea, but once it had arrived, there was no clearing it from my mind. And I'd already agreed to do it, anyway. "I haven't given you that massage yet."

She wasn't moving, but she seemed to go even more still. With her eyes trained on my bare feet, she said, "That'd... be nice."

"Come on." I successfully sounded like it was no big deal, even as my brain and body waged in an all-out war. I was going to have my hands on her skin. It was exactly where my hands should not go if I was going to keep my lust for her somewhere near manageable.

But manageability was already proving to be a problem.

I strategically turned as I stood to conceal my semi. She took the hand I extended to help her to her feet, then followed me down the short hallway to my bedroom. Without pausing, I went into the bathroom and found the massage oil on the counter next to the sink. I took the opportunity to adjust my cock more securely down my pant leg.

When I stepped back into the other room, Emmeline was pushing her leggings down her legs, revealing a pair of biking shorts. Somehow, they were even thinner than her leggings had been.

"What are you doing?" My voice rumbling lower and huskier than just moments before, making it clear this was, in fact, a big fucking deal.

She paused, half bent over, showcasing her ripe, firm ass. "I was stretching on the floor. My clothes are covered in dog hair, and I didn't want to get it on your bed."

"Shit, right. The dog hair is a lot. Sorry."

Standing, she met my eye. "Oh my god, don't worry about it."

"I'll wash your clothes."

She rolled her eyes. "I'll wash my own clothes." Then she pulled her T-shirt over her head, leaving her in just a sports bra and those little fucking shorts.

*God. Damn.*

I clenched my jaw to keep it from dropping open.

Her lower lip sucked into her mouth and a blush rose up her chest. "I haven't shaved, so don't look at my legs."

I scoffed, "Em, I could give a fuck."

"Because we're so platonic?" Her chest stilled as if she was holding her breath.

I swallowed and shook my head.

She pinched her lips together, but I saw the smile toying with her lips.

My heartbeat thundered in my ear. "Lay down."

She knelt at the edge of the bed first before going to all fours. It felt like she moved slowly, though it was probably just my new perception of time. I hadn't known that a second could take so long as she lowered to lie on her stomach. Her elbows bent at her shoulders, defining the soft lines of muscles under her skin. And her round, perfect ass was just right there.

"Like this?" Her voice sounded a little breathy.

Fuck, this was working too well for me.

*Fuck.*

"Here." I reached for my pillow. "Lay on this."

She took it and went to put it under her head.

"No." I stopped her. "Under your torso."

Over her shoulder, she gave me a confused look.

I smirked. "On your hands and knees."

When she was up, I placed the pillow so her pelvis would be slightly lifted and her neck would stretch toward the comforter. Then, with my palm flat on the small of her back, I gently eased her down, her skin hot and smooth beneath my touch.

"Just like that."

She was compliant, which fed into my desires just right. She waited for me to touch her—to make her feel good—but this wasn't everything my head was making it out to be. My only permission was to massage oil on her back and shoulders, and all the other thoughts in my mind needed to quiet themselves.

I stood at the edge of the bed and squirted the oil onto my hand. The smell of wintergreen filled my nose.

She sighed. "That smells so good."

I rubbed my palms together. "I like it, too."

Her ribs expanded with a quick breath when I placed my hands on her shoulder blades.

"Too cold?" I asked.

"No, it's good." Even as close as we were, I could barely hear her whisper.

There was a void of emotion in her voice that made me uncomfortable. "Do you want me to stop?"

"Don't stop."

My semi stiffened and my jaw tightened. My hands worked the oil over her skin and I watched her eyelids drift closed as my thumbs stroked along her neck. I couldn't hear her sigh, instead I felt it rumble against my touch.

I watched my hands move across her back, dazed at the sight. Her muscles grew pliable under my ministrations. The partial fulfillment of my fantasies only made me more aware of her every breath. She giggled when I grazed her ribs.

"Ticklish?" I grinned.

"Yes."

After a while her back shone, and I'd touched every inch of her I was allowed to.

Stepping back, I worked the excess oil into my neck. "I'm going to change and take care of that stuff at work. You don't have to come if you want to stay."

"You don't want me to come?" There was a relaxed thickness in her voice.

*I definitely want you to come... over and over again.*

"If you want to, I'd like that. You just look... comfortable. If you wanna rest—"

"It's tempting." She sighed and pushed herself up. "But I want to see your work. Can we pet some dogs?"

"What? I don't have enough for you?"

"There can always be more dogs."

I lifted an eyebrow.

"Not here." She swiped her hands through the air and looked up at me from the edge of my bed. "You have reached maximum dog capacity here."

Her messy bun atop her head had gotten even messier. She looked comfortable sitting there, her eyes a little heavy. I liked making her look satisfied and rumpled.

We needed to get away from this bed.

"Then let's go. Maybe I can convince you to adopt Journey." I turned my back to grab a pair of jeans from my dresser.

"Who's Journey?"

"She's a Great Dane, and so sweet. She gets seizures if she goes off her medications, so no one will take her home because of her health issues."

"Let's go meet Journey, then."

***

Emmeline turned her head to read the MacIntosh Dog Shelter sign as I steered into the drive.

"MacIntosh... Is this owned by Bill MacIntosh?"

I nodded.

"Oh shit, Bill MacIntosh is your boss? Can you get me a meeting?"

"A meeting?"

Her eyes were wide and bright. "Yeah, I've been trying to meet with him to get some of his rental business. If I could just get a face-to-face... He's hardly ever around and when he is, loads of salespeople are trying to get his time and I'm just white noise. If you could help me get a meeting, that'd be amazing."

I scrubbed the back of my neck. "I don't really know him."

"I totally get it. But you do know him, right?"

"A little." I pinched my fingers together. "There's a holiday potluck at his place every year."

"Potluck? He doesn't have it catered?"

"It's more homey if everyone brings a dish to pass, I guess."

Her eyebrows drew together.

"And I normally don't mix my personal life and work."

Her shoulders sagged, but she nodded. "That's cool, I get it."

We drove past the kennel building, the individually fenced outdoor runs lining its exterior were empty—the dogs had obviously decided that temperatures hovering around zero were too damn cold. I glanced at the main parking lot, and seeing staff and volunteers' cars parked there, I parked outside the medical building—I was hoping we may be able to avoid my coworkers.

Ella lumbered inside as quickly as she could—she had a little hitch in her step, possibly from an ache in her hip.

"Are you worried?" Emmeline asked, pushing her hood. If she was still disappointed, she didn't show it.

I shrugged. "No... maybe. Ella's getting less mobile. If I have to adjust her treatment or exercise, I want to do it now."

Em watched me, her eyes growing soft. "Let's get it figured out, then."

It turned out she was a great motivator for Ella to be still for her X-rays and to do a couple new exercises. I didn't want to cause more pain, so we went light; I was more interested in stretches. The X-rays showed that her arthritis wasn't worse, and I didn't want to increase her pain medication for fear that it'd upset her stomach or kidneys. We'd do more stretching at home. The cold weather was probably giving her flares.

"Hey, doc," Molly, one of our vet techs, said from the entrance of the examination room.

Ella's harrumph went ignored as Molly gasped, her silvering braid swung off her shoulder in her excitement. "Oh my god! Are you his wife?"

A blush rose on Emmeline's face, but she smiled. "That's me."

"I'm Molly. It's so exciting to meet you. He wouldn't even tell us your name! I was beginning to think you weren't real." Soft wrinkles formed in the corners of her brown eyes as she grinned.

I coughed, somewhere between shock and humor.

Emmeline's laugh burst out. "I'm mostly real."

I shook my head at her near-truth.

Taking Molly's hand, Em shook it. "It's nice to meet you. This guy is so tight-lipped, I'm surprised he told you about me at all."

I gathered a couple of heating pads from the cupboards while they talked. "Moll, do you mind if I put Ella in your office? I want Em to meet Journey."

"Sure."

I got my big dog situated with the pads on her hips. She laid her head back on the edge of the dog bed.

As I approached the examination room, I heard Molly ask, "So, he was like, 'Meet me in Vegas,' and you just... did?"

"Kinda. Honestly, I've never fallen this hard for someone in my life."

My brain tried to convince my heart not to take her words as truth—they were for the sake of our story and nothing more. I'd never fallen for anyone the way I'd fallen for her. It hadn't taken very long, and now I was free falling without a net.

"I would think not," Molly agreed.

"It's just kinda been a free fall..."

I swallowed at Emmeline's words echoing my thoughts.

"Like, I never would have thought I'd... *elope*. I don't know, it just felt right."

"Hmm, love is strange, huh?"

"So strange."

My heart wedged into my throat as I came back into the examination room. "Ready to meet Journey?"

"Sure." She slipped her hand into mine, like it belonged there. Like we held hands all the time. Like it wasn't for Molly's benefit.

*But it was.*

"Will I see you at the open house?" she asked.

"Absolutely." Em beamed. "That's the best part of not being secret anymore. I get to start coming to these things."

# CHAPTER 14

## EMMELINE

I thought getting out of the house would help with my all-consuming need for Owen, but it hadn't. He'd been careful and attentive with Ella; his voice warm with gentle encouragement. Her brown eyes lit up with affection and trust for him. It was too endearing.

Then I met Journey, who was also in love with him. She was on the small side for a Great Dane, or so Owen claimed, but a one-hundred-pound dog was still rather large. As soon as I met her, she leaned all her weight against my thigh and wagged her tail, looking up at me with a goofy smile.

I wasn't planning on getting a dog, but I was questioning whether or not I should.

Back at his house, I completed my bedtime routine and entered his bedroom. Owen was propped against his headboard with a book on his lap.

My mind conjured the shiver-inducing memory of his hands running over my skin. His breath warm and steady against my flesh. His directions clear and firm, opening a desire I hadn't known I had.

*We're just friends,* I repeated to myself. But every time I did, I heard Laurie scoff in my head.

He looked up, then his eyes dropped to my bare legs—still un-shaven.

*Em, I could give a fuck.*

And just like that, the *we're just friends* mantra was obliterated.

I was not feeling very friendly toward him.

Not at all.

Judging by the way he swallowed, he wasn't feeling so friendly toward me, either.

The only sound in the room was from my feet padding on the floor as I rounded his bed. I took my hair out of the clip at the back of my head. It felt intimate... lurid, almost like I was undressing for him. I didn't shake my hair out or anything, but it was implied. Kinda.

He'd looked back at his book, but it didn't seem to hold his focus. Just like how I kept him in my peripheral vision as I lifted the covers and slid under them.

I nestled into my pillow, then rolled onto my side away from the lamp lit on his bedside table. It was the only solution to how badly I wanted to just watch him; how badly I wanted to take in the view and fully appreciate his beauty.

*Just my friend.* It was a total lie.

Behind me, there was a soft thud and then the click of the light.

He shifted to lay down as I rolled back to face him. The sharp lower line of his jaw was illuminated by the soft moonlight filtering in from the window. How was a jawbone so attractive? I swallowed. "You can keep reading."

"It's cool. I was done anyway," he said to the ceiling.

I laid on my back as well, staring up at nothing in particular. My attention was still on him, and an ache grew more intense low in my belly.

Outside, the wind blew the snow sideways, piling drifts like sand in the desert.

Inside, liquid fire coursed through my veins.

The edge of his pinky touched mine and all that heat had somewhere to go. A half inch of skin on skin. An accident.

Flames.

It was a very nice half inch of skin—probably the best half inch on any human body ever. And it just made me more curious. What other discoveries could I make about his body's terrain? There must be somewhere else on him that I'd like even better. Would it be under my lips where his pulse beat against his throat? Or at the tips of my fingers trailing a line down his sides? Or would it be the insides of my thighs wrapped around his hips?

His pinky curled, leaving me without for only a second before it drew a line from my second knuckle to my nail and back. I held my breath, and next to me, Owen held his.

At this point, oxygen was a distraction. I would survive on breaths of Owen from now on.

I hovered my hand above the back of his. The pad of my fingertip stroked down the length of his middle finger—and I found even more of his perfect skin.

My heart raced, aroused beyond any reasonable explanation. When he looked back at me, raw desire burned in his gaze.

Propped on his elbow, he tentatively reached his hand to my face. His fingers were strong as he cupped my jaw and stroked his thumb along the edge of my lower lip.

"Emmeline..." he whispered.

"Owen." My tongue wet my lips, barely brushing the end of his thumb. He groaned. His fingers flexed. Instinctively, my back arched—a silent plea for his hand to move down.

I gripped his wrist, and his pulse jumped a quick beat against my grip.

The distance between our mouths closed as he leaned over me, and just like our New Year's Eve kiss, it began slow, just barely a sweep of contact. We explored with tentative movements. I brushed my hand into the hair at the base of his neck. He sucked my lip between his teeth. But unlike that first kiss, this one didn't stop.

It grew.

It trapped time.

It swelled until it was the only reality I'd ever known.

Every electrical signal from my brain was in exultation of finally kissing Owen.

His tongue plunged deep and urgent as my fingers curled in his hair. I hooked my knee around his hip and ground into him, already hard against my heat.

"Tell me what you want." His words were warm puffs against my skin as he drew the tip of his nose along my neck until my ear was between his teeth. His heart pounded against my chest. The muscles of his forearm jumped under my palm.

"Please," I begged.

"Please, what? I need this to be good for you." There was a tethered edge to his voice, something barely restrained, and it only pushed me further from my own control. Everything that would come next was inevitable, even if it wasn't something either of us had planned.

Spontaneous inevitability.

"It will be." I sucked on his neck, needing to taste more of him.

I was completely drenched in the scent of wintergreen and his skin, the same way I had been all day. His lips brushed my earlobe once more, and I shuddered. I ground against him again, putting pressure against my swollen clit, but the ache was still there.

I was dizzy with it.

"I appreciate the confidence."

I twisted the white cotton on his back in my fist, and he pushed up to look me in the eye. "I feel like I've been edging for a year for you. This isn't a one-time thing for me."

"Good. Me either." I pushed up to kiss him again, but he pulled away too quickly.

"Then tell me what you like." His hands slipped under the hem of my shorts and squeezed my bare ass. "I'll give you anything, Em."

If I didn't believe him, the intensity and dark promise in his hazel eyes would have made the truth of his words obvious.

"Please, just more. Let's have fun." I shivered at the scrape of his teeth on my jaw.

"I like fun."

I giggled. "I do, too."

He ground against me once, his hard cock pressed right where I needed him. We made matching sounds of appreciation, savoring the feel of our bodies finding something nearing what they needed. It was like we were finally feeding a deprivation we'd weathered for weeks or months—or maybe my entire life, because nothing and no one lit me on fire like Owen did.

He marked a trail down my chest with soft bites. "Can you do me a favor and tell me when I do something fun?" I heard the smile in his voice.

"Sure—"

But the word was cut short when his mouth found my nipple over my shirt and sucked. Sensations ricocheted inside of me as I gasped. The layer of clothing should have desensitized me, yet I was over-whelmed by him.

"That," I cried. "That's fun!"

A laugh rumbled in his chest. His palms slipped under my shirt, bunching it under my arms, and lifting it out of his way.

I truly fell apart.

I rolled my hips into him.

He was so hard.

When he hummed, "Mmm-hm," before moving to my other nipple, I realized I'd said, *So hard* out loud.

"Is this still fun, Em?"

"Yes." My hips rocked unconsciously.

I wanted more and everything, and for him to keep doing whatever he was doing to me forever.

My nipple slipped from his lips with a *pop*. He slid his teeth along my ribcage, which would normally tickle, but I was too aroused to notice.

"Fuck," I gasped.

He paused near my belly button and tilted his head to meet my eye. "I always imagined you talking." He hooked an arm around my thigh and gripped my hip. He lazily stroked between my leg and lips. "You telling me everything you want me to do to you."

"You're chattier than I thought." When I realized what I'd said, I added, "It's not bad." I laughed. "Sorry, I'm not very good at this."

Above my quivering stomach, his laugh was throatier than usual. "Not from where I'm at."

I sucked in a sharp breath when he bit and sucked high on my inner thigh.

"You're *really* fucking good at this. Like, what the fuck are you doing to me?"

"Having fun." He bent his head and licked where his fingers had just been.

His glossy black hair tickled my stomach.

Wrapping his arm around my thigh, he urged my knees further apart. He hooked the crotch of my shorts in one finger and pulled them to the side. His knuckle slid against my clit, and I moaned in the back of my throat. He kissed his way to the coarse curls atop my mound, while he ran a finger up and down my slick slit. I couldn't stop my hips from shifting.

Instinct drove me.

Instinct to come—to finally find release at his hand, his mouth, his cock.

"Please, Owen," I begged.

"Please what, Em?" He kept kissing and biting and sucking, but not deeper than my lips. Two of his fingers pressed circles low on my mound, and it was almost enough.

"Make me come."

"How?"

"I don't care."

From below my stomach, he tilted his head in a playful challenge. "Oh, I think you do."

"Your mouth," I whispered.

He nuzzled his cheek against my leg. The challenge was gone from his eyes, replaced by something softer. "Are you feeling shy?"

"A little."

"Am I pushing you too far?"

I shook my head. "It's kinda fun."

Dimples pressed deep into his cheeks as he smiled. He ran a finger along my drenched slit and circled my clit. "I like fun."

All I could do was bite my lip and nod.

He repeated the circle. "You seem to think this is fun."

"Yes."

"But you want my mouth."

"Please."

"Anything, Em." And then pressure from the flat of his tongue made me grind against his face. My fists twisted in the sheets. His fingers delved inside of me, pushing up on my walls until my legs shook and I cried out. He sucked and licked and urged—pressure mounting.

I writhed and begged, "Please," over and over.

Orgasms weren't generally challenging for me to achieve, but the speed of this one shocked me, overwhelmed me. My skin was made of electricity. My blood rushed in my ears, and my eyes were squeezed tight. He laid kisses on my mound and pelvis as I shivered.

When my breathing finally settled, I said, "That was very fun."

He smiled against my stomach.

It must have been the empowering rush of ecstasy, but I wasn't feeling very shy anymore. "Take off your clothes."

Pushing up, he knelt between my thighs. He held my gaze and lifted the hem of his shirt up, revealing tan skin over tight muscles. The lines of his collarbones were sharp above rounded pectorals. A V at his hips disappeared under his shorts, like an arrow directing my eyes.

I sat and ran a hand up the bisected line of his abs. His head fell back as I circled his dark nipple with my thumb.

"It's a public service that you don't run shirtless." I punctuated my sentence with a kiss on his stomach. His erection bounced against my chest. "You could cause accidents."

"You think it's better with you in your sports bra? You're a god-damn menace."

"A *menace*?" My hands slipped around his back and lower, to the waistband of his shorts. I gripped the elastic and pulled down the back, slipping my fingers over the curve of his ass. I trailed kisses, scraping the edge of my teeth to the center of his body. I wasn't usually much for biting, but he seemed to be, and it was making me a bit wild.

He slipped a hand into my hair. The rise and fall of his chest was quick and shallow. A muscle twitched in his jaw.

The slippery material of his shorts slid down his hips. The V at his hips grew narrower and narrower until I forgot all about it, because every inch that his shorts slipped down revealed another inch of his cock. I pushed them to his knees, and his hard length pressed between my breasts. I ran my hands up the back of his thighs, digging my nails in as I grabbed his round ass.

With a guiding pull of my hair, he lay me on the bed. He gripped the sheets over my head with white knuckles as his bicep flexed and released.

"Do you have a condom?" I reached between us to squeeze his cock.

His hips bucked into my hand.

I continued working him, relishing the precum dripping onto my stomach. He stretched for his bedside table and opened the drawer. A moment later he knelt again, leaving my hand empty. With his eyes trained on me, he tore the wrapper open with his teeth and rolled it down his length. He stood and pushed his shorts the rest of the way down while I shimmied mine off, as well as my shirt.

Our eyes met for only a moment before I looked away. Partially to take in the sight of him naked and hard, but also because in that moment, I felt more bare than my naked body. I pushed all those emotions to the side and focused on the enjoyment. The heat. The fun.

Not the demanding way my heart ached in my chest.

He placed his tip at my entrance before he slowly pushed inside—watching my face the whole time.

A moan sighed from between my lips.

Our hips rolled together. A patient slip in and out, replaced with growing urgency. As my movements came faster and more insistent, he met them stroke for stroke until the sound of our skin smacking joined our moans.

I flexed around him as he hit a spot deep inside me again and again.

I sighed his name over and over—a thank you and a plea. His body drove me closer to my second release.

Two of his fingers pressed low on my mound again.

My face trapped on the "O" at the beginning of his name, but no sound came out as wave after wave crashed through my body.

"Goddamn, you're fucking hot." His thrusts became less rhythmic and more punishing. "So hot, and tight, and wet."

Through the fog of my orgasm, I devoured the bunching of his pecs and biceps, the muscle jumping in his jaw as he neared his climax. His fingers dug harder into my ass, his strength taking over his normal gentleness. Then he plunged into me, his abs flexed as he spilled into the condom.

We stayed like that for a few gasping breaths.

One at a time, his fingers loosened on my ass. The press of his forehead on my shoulder eased away. The distance between our bodies grew in increments until he pulled out of me and stood. He walked on legs that looked slightly unreliable to dispose of the condom in the bathroom waste bin.

When he curled against my back under the sheets, a contented sigh slipped from my lips. I shifted more securely against him. "That was fun... Let's do it again."

"Right now? Or..."

My eyes were already closed. I shifted my hips to snuggle closer to him. "Sleep first."

He kissed my shoulder and something tender bloomed in my chest. "Good night, Em."

"Good night."

# CHAPTER 15

## EMMELINE

The mall post-holidays was always a strange adjustment, with winter decorations on display—giant green wreathes with red poinsettias on them—and non-holiday music playing over the speakers. Maybe that was why I felt a little off walking next to Owen under the bright florescent lights.

The days had gone by quickly. Somehow, the entire week had passed, and Owen's open house was tomorrow. Every night we went to bed sated and satisfied, and most mornings we woke up naked, his cock hard and nestled against my ass. Our alarms would go off, demanding that we start our day while he was inside of me, both of us climbing to release.

For the most part, my coworkers had been excited and full of questions, not to mention invitations to dinners and parties that, as a single woman, I hadn't received. Carl, on the other hand, had given me a convincing smile and said, "I can't believe you're married."

"I know, it was all very sudden," I answered.

"No, I mean, I don't believe it."

We were leaning against the dispatch counter close enough to Sam and Lewis that they glanced over toward us.

Heat rose up my cheeks, my stupid pale skin giving away my nerves. "Why would you say that?"

"I'm your neighbor. I've never seen this guy—"

"*This guy*, my husband, is named Owen," I interrupted. "And if you're paying that close of attention to me, Carl, then I suggest closing your blinds."

He opened his mouth, but he was cut off by Sam, of all people, "Why the accusations?"

"I just don't believe it," Carl argued.

"Go take care of that Drexel order and leave Em alone," Lewis directed.

Carl plastered on his friendly smile and walked away.

Lewis leaned toward me. "Just ignore him, Em."

"I always do," I replied, sounding more confident than I felt.

That was the thing about lies; under scrutiny, they fell apart.

Owen and I strode past one of my favorite discount home decor stores. I resisted the urge to ask him to step in for candles because I knew I'd end up wandering and perusing. At home, I lit candles and drank tea and read in bed. It was the only part of my normal routine I missed.

It hadn't even been a week yet. There was still time for Owen and me to grow sick of each other.

But I couldn't really see that happening.

I liked being at Owen's. The dogs made things interesting, up to and including that Venice ate anything left out—explaining the list of items next to his name on the Puppy Wellness Chart. I'd started joining Owen and Bandit on evening runs, with either Venice or Indie as my jogging buddy—though I wasn't committed enough to get out of Owen's warm bed to run in the freezing cold mornings. Even Maui allowed me to pet Ella this morning.

Then, of course, there was Owen and his dry wit. And the whole friends-with-benefits thing was working like a goddamn charm. I had never been so satisfied... ever.

My body knew his in a molecular way.

We thrummed on the same frequency.

And he smelled so fucking good all the fucking time. I had to stop chewing wintergreen gum because I'd formed an erotic response to it.

The first jewelry store we neared had a sign reading: Up to 20% off. I didn't bother to look up at the name of the place. If I thought about it, I'd probably know which franchise it was just from passing it hundreds of times over the years.

But I was keeping my thoughts on a surface level.

I turned in first, walking like a woman on a mission—a mission to purchase a wedding ring for a fake marriage.

My life was very odd.

There were a couple of other people milling about, and the salespeople were preoccupied with them.

Side by side, Owen and I stood at the entrance, where the tile of the mall floor switched to the store's worn pink carpet. Just a few feet away, well-lit glass counters acted as cases for gleaming jewelry.

"Huh." Owen's jaw muscle flexed. "I guess we should have talked about this, but, uh, what sort of... Is there something you have in mind?"

"A ring?"

He blinked at me, a little annoyed. "Yes, but what kind?"

I blinked back, a little annoyed as well. "The kind that goes on my finger."

"Are you being purposefully difficult?"

"I don't know how I could be any more clear."

"Hello, can I help you?" a middle-aged woman asked. Over her right breast, a name tag read Renee. Her hair was curled and sprayed into submission, and the smile on her face was lined in bright pink lipstick.

"Hi, we're looking for a wedding band," I answered. I glanced down at the gold ring already wrapped around Owen's finger. Did it feel unnatural to wear it? Would it feel like the lie it was when I had one on my hand, too?

"Congratulations! When's the big day?"

"We eloped." I naturally matched her enthusiasm, even though I was nervous and kind of irritated and feeling... off.

"How romantic!"

The fact that Owen and I were standing a couple of feet apart and not touching at all didn't deter her excitement.

"What do you have in mind?" she asked.

"Just a basic gold band."

"So, you could be more clear," he muttered under his breath.

I lifted an eyebrow in his direction as I followed her. When she was a few feet ahead of us, on the other side of the counter, I whispered, "Is everything okay?"

"Yeah, sorry." He sighed. "I'm kinda on edge."

"Me, too. This is super bizarre, right?"

He gave me a half smile. "Yeah, a little."

"We're okay, though, right? Like, this can be weird, but we're good?"

His hand was a little damp when he squeezed mine. "We're okay."

I considered him for a moment before I nodded. "Let's go do this."

"Okay."

The selection process only took a few minutes. I spotted a basic gold band, the price tags facing up. "That one will do."

Renee's pencil-darkened eyebrows shot up. "A woman who knows her mind. I see why you married her."

"She's unlike anyone else." His agreement unlocked a cage in my chest. The nerves in my stomach turned into butterflies, fluttering on delicate wings.

A blush rose on his tan skin.

Her eyes went gooey. "I can see why this union works." She pointed to me. "What size do you need?"

I rattled off my size. My finger was slightly larger than most sample sizes.

She held the ring toward Owen. "You two didn't have a ring ceremony?"

The little band sat in the middle of his hand. We shared a glance and shrugged before shaking our heads.

"Well, then. Give her your ring," she directed him.

His forehead wrinkled as he glanced between me and her. I shook my head, not having any idea what was going on either.

She nodded with encouragement. "It'll be worth it."

Still confused, he eased the band off his finger.

"Now give it to her." She pointed a bright pink fingernail toward me.

I held my hand palm up and he dropped the ring into my hand, the gold slightly warm from his skin.

"You go first," she directed me.

"Go first?" I asked.

"I'm sorry, I'm messing this up. You put his ring on him, and then he'll put your ring on you." She folded her hands on the glass-top and waited, as if the store wasn't bustling around us.

Holding out my hand, I waited for him to give me his left. Why were my palms sweating? Could he tell? But once his hand was in mine, I didn't care. His fingers were slender, with bold knuckles and clean, short nails. For the past couple of days, those hands had traveled my body and found all the places I liked to be touched.

This union was fake, but those hands' knowledge was very real.

They knew me.

He knew me.

And that was where the ache settled, where the nervous energy sprang from. My heart that pumped through each day was falling harder and harder for him.

But how could a relationship withstand the pressure of starting like this? With every person we knew thinking we had already passed the finish line when we hadn't even started the race.

Was it really so impossible for us to get past this?

I looked up to find him watching me, his head tilted and his eyes pensive.

The gold band slipped over his knuckles and fit nicely against his skin. He took a moment to consider it before he took my left hand in his, then slowly pushed the ring up. The tips of his fingers stayed in place, just after my knuckle, where the ring stopped. It was a little too small.

But just barely.

And now that he'd been the one to put it there, I didn't want to take it off.

"That was lovely," Renee said in a watery voice. She patted under her eyes. "Sorry, I'm a terrible romantic. It's just so clear how much you love each other."

"Oh my goodness, you are so sweet." I smiled at her—and she was—but inside, I was fully freaking out. What just happened? Why did it feel like I could feel the tips of his fingers gently cradle my heart?

The butterflies and their fragile wings were trapped in the whirlwind of my chest.

We left wearing the rings. It would have taken a week to get my size in, and by then, I'd only have it for a little while before tucking it inside my jewelry box, hiding away whatever this moment of my life was forever.

The realization made my throat feel tight.

"You're being quiet," he observed. His stride matched mine, which apparently, was very quick.

"You're quiet all the time."

"Yeah, but that's my normal. It's unsettling when you're quiet. Are we okay?"

I stopped to face him. "No."

His eyebrows lifted, waiting for me to speak.

The silence stretched on, and I didn't know how to articulate my thoughts—my feelings. "I need candles."

"Okay. Where do we get these candles?"

I pointed to HomeGoods.

"Perfect, let's get candles." He grabbed my hand and took a step but stopped when I didn't move.

"And… I *really* like you."

A crooked smile pushed a dimple into his cheek. "I *really* like you, too."

"No, I like, *really* like you."

He gripped my hips and pulled me close enough to plant a kiss on my forehead. "I like, *really* like you, too."

"What does that mean, though?" I whispered. "Like this is… Owen, I just bought a wedding band. This is so *weird*."

He laughed. "It is."

It must have been contagious, because I started laughing. With our foreheads pressed together, we laughed like we were alone and not in the middle of the mall. After a few moments, we pulled apart, still smiling and shaking our heads.

"I don't know. I don't know how to make this normal, but I like you." He tugged on my hand. "Come on, let's go get you some candles."

I picked out five candles, and Owen bought a shelf to keep them away from Indie's reach. Every once in a while, we'd make eye contact and start laughing again. In the checkout lane, I grabbed a box of my mom's favorite chocolate-covered cookies without thinking, but then I set them back. I'd texted her earlier asking how she and Dad were, and she'd said they were fine. I had thought that was the end of the conversation—if it could even be called that—but an hour or so later, she texted asking how things were with me and Owen. My response of, **Great, thanks for asking**, was the actual end of the conversation.

But it was something.

Because neither of us were in the mood to cook, Owen and I ordered take-out. While we sat in the vinyl chairs waiting for our food, I looked up from my phone screen to see Carl and his wife Trisha. He had the look of someone pretending not to recognize someone else.

I shifted in my seat to face Owen. Gently brushing his hair off his forehead, I waited for his eyes to meet mine. "I need you to kiss me."

He looked down at my lips. "Okay."

"My coworker is over there—*don't look*—and he gave me shit, saying he didn't think we were married. So I need you to kiss me."

He was still watching my mouth. "You could have stopped at, 'I need you to kiss me.'"

My cheeks warmed. "Are you saying you want to?"

"*Desperately.*"

My eyelids fluttered closed as his mouth pressed against mine. Somewhere in the kitchen, metal hit metal. There was the buzz of conversation. The world kept spinning, but in that moment with Owen, everything else drifted into fuzzy focus, and at the same time, he came into sharper focus. His fingers trailed in my hair as he sucked my lower lip. He tugged all the strings of my heart tight. My hand pressed against the heart beating in his chest, and I sent out a silent plea for it to feel as tied up in me as mine was in his. That those ties could remain unbroken.

I didn't notice the hostess return, and judging by the blush on her face, it had taken a minute for Owen to notice as well.

The car ride home was full of the scent of Chinese food and my hand clasped in his, even though there was no one there to see it.

Instead of joining Bandit and Owen on their jog, I lit my candles and read a book, Venice's head resting on my thigh.

After his shower, Owen slipped into bed. The smell of wintergreen and extinguished flame mingled in my half-sleeping brain. He wrapped himself around my back, his knees fitting into the pocket behind mine.

"You're still good to come with me to that appreciation dinner, right?" I asked.

He kissed my bare shoulder. "I said I would."

"Thank you."

The ring on his left hand slid against mine as he snuggled closer to me.

A sigh rumbled in my chest, contented.

His breathing grew longer and the arm around my waist grew heavier. I sank into sleep with him. My thoughts were hazy around the edges, and the line between consciousness and subconsciousness grew blurry.

My eyes sprang open as he sleepily muttered, "How are we going to end this?"

# CHAPTER 16

## OWEN

By the time Emmeline arrived at the MacIntosh Dog Shelter open house, the excitement of her impending presence was a buzz among my coworkers. Dutch coaxed the energy by telling every stranger in attendance that I was his nephew-in-law and that his beautiful niece would be here any minute. I wanted to shy away from the attention, but there wasn't much I could do. I was trapped behind a table full of T-shirts with the shelter's logo on it for the next hour.

People really seemed to like the story though, and Dutch liked to talk, which made my role easier. All I needed to contribute was a smile and a nod, and they were happy to hear the retelling of the New Year's Eve party and how Dutch had put it all together.

I should have known he wouldn't sink into silence when it was just the two of us.

"How's married life treatin' ya, Owen?"

"Good," I answered, surprised that it wasn't false, even if the marriage was. I really did like living with Em. It was corny, but I liked starting and ending my days seeing her. "How about you? How's married life?"

A gooey grin filled his face. "Aw, brother, it just gets better."

Rearranging the stacks of shirts, I kept my face turned away from him. His earnestness made me feel even more guilty for lying to him.

Volunteers milled about with our more docile dogs on leashes—each with tongues lulled out and enjoying the attention they received from strangers.

"I hear you're having dinner at Simon and Vivian's tonight."

I nodded.

"I knew they'd come around, just a little shocked, is all. They'll see Em's got a good one."

"Look at that, two of my favorite people." I looked up and took in the sight of Emmeline in jeans and a navy T-shirt like the ones on display. The fit emphasized her athletic build and stopped right at the fullness of her hips. The ways my body reacted to her was unreasonable. My stomach dropped like I was going down a steep hill. My heart quickened. She liked me—she'd told me so—but I still couldn't quite believe it, especially not after so many months of believing my feelings were one-sided.

My greeting was swallowed up by Dutch's exclamation, "There she is!"

She laughed and responded to him, but looked at me. "Here I am."

There were only eight people or so in the medical building, but they all watched us. I couldn't be normal under their eyes. I shoved my hands into my pockets, not knowing what to do with them.

"How'd you get the shirt?" I asked.

"I called Dutch earlier this week and he helped me out. You like it?"

"I do."

"Sweetheart, why don't you take my place? I'm gonna get us some hotdogs." Putting a hand on my shoulder, Dutch squeezed. "I'm sure he'd like your company better than mine."

Everyone was still watching, and the scrutiny seemed to be affecting her, too. She ducked her head so even I couldn't see her expression.

I put my hand on her hip and moved in to kiss her, at the same time she went to give me a hug and rest her head on my shoulder. We moved like puppets, with jerky starts and stops. She turned and met my lips, but our mouths connected too quickly. Our teeth scraped together. She pulled back, her eyes cast to the tile floor.

"Sorry about that," I whispered near her ear.

She shrugged. "It's fine. Just timing."

Tilting my head, I tried to see her face. She'd slept curled around her pillow, as if she was trying to take up as little space as possible. I'd left for work before she had woken up—at least, that was how it looked. I had a feeling that she was awake and pretending to be asleep.

During my jog with Bandit, I'd picked up my thoughts from the night before. Looking at the situation from every angle, I wondered how we could end this lie and proceed with a real relationship. She had branded me. Her kiss was a sear on my lips, as if kissing had never existed before my mouth found hers. All other kisses were a shadow and hers was the sun. Every few minutes I'd get a shiver down my spine, remembering her heat and taste and touch. I wanted more.

A lot more.

Not just more nights.

I wanted *everything*.

It was exciting to want after so many years of not trusting myself to. Not trusting that I could be *the one* for someone. Not trusting that the rug wouldn't be pulled out from underneath me.

"Want me to try again?" I joked.

"I think once was enough."

She sounded normal enough, but something didn't feel right—more than a bad kiss could account for.

"Is everything okay?"

"Of course." She met my eye almost like a challenge. "What would be wrong?"

I shook my head. "I don't know." I wanted to push the subject, but Molly was approaching with our volunteer coordinator Mandi. The two middle-aged women wore matching excited expressions.

"Emmeline, it's so good to see you!" Molly made introductions.

The strange vibes ebbed, but they didn't slip away entirely. When I entwined my fingers with Em, she squeezed back. I thought we were past the point where I would have to wonder if she held my hand because she wanted to or because people were around. But it didn't feel that way.

Dutch strode back, carrying two hotdogs in each hand. "Don't they look good together?"

Em and I shared embarrassed glances as everyone else looked at us like adorable puppies. Well, I looked embarrassed; Emmeline looked indulgent.

She took a hotdog from her uncle, then she jerked her head outside of our group. "That couple has spent a lot of time with Journey."

"Maybe she'll find a home." Mandi crossed her red-tipped fingers.

My heart twisted, hoping it was true.

A volunteer walked up, and after mumbling something to Mandi and Molly, the three of them walked away with a wave.

"Have you heard any more about MacIntosh being in town?" Em asked her uncle.

Dutch shook his head. "I'll let you know if I do, though."

She'd accepted that I liked to keep my work and personal life separate and hadn't asked for my help again. I'd actually forgotten it was something she wanted...

*Maybe I could—*

A spike of anxiety cut that thought off.

***

"We're just gonna walk right in?" I asked.

Emmeline looked over her shoulder at me. "What else would we do? I mean, it's my parents' house. It'd be hella strange if I knocked on the door." She punched in a code to unlock the deadbolt to their garage.

When I pictured our arrival, I imagined we would go to the front door and knock—even though it would be unnatural for me to knock on my parents' door.

We entered the heated four-car garage and walked around a new SUV, a large new truck, and a sleek-looking car under a cover. I wasn't a car guy, but I'd guessed that the contents of this garage alone cost more than the value of my house.

We'd been shocked by her mom's call the night before, and even more shocked by the dinner invitation.

"You okay?" Em asked.

I lifted my eyebrows and nodded.

She paused in front of the door. "They're good people, Owen. They wouldn't invite us if they weren't ready to... mend things."

I placed my hand on her hip. There'd been a distance between us all day that I didn't understand. She said everything was fine, and all I couldn't tell if she was lying or if my trust issues were surfacing.

She stared through my chest, and I had to tilt my head to meet her eyes. "I'm sure they are good people."

I didn't know what else to say; instead, I eased her toward me wrapping one of my arms around her back.

That was how her dad found us when he opened the door.

He straightened and blinked, not expecting us to be at the door.

We separated, and she smoothed her hair behind her ear. "Dad, hey."

"I didn't hear you two come in."

"We just did."

He released his hold. "I was gonna grab a beer, you want one?"

"Does Mom have wine picked out?"

He squinted, and I recognized the sarcastic expression from seeing a version of it on her face.

"I'll drink the wine."

"Owen, would you like a beer?" It looked like he had to brace himself to look at me, a slight broadening of his shoulders.

"No, thank you, I'm driving."

He jerked his head in a nod.

He nodded, then he held his arms. "C'mere, sweetheart."

She hugged her dad back, a quick embrace.

We stood like three awkward statues for a few moments. Em thawed first, leaning down to slip her boots off. It was like a switch flipped back to 'On.' I stepped to the side to let her dad through to the fridge just inside the garage.

The mudroom entered into a kitchen where I was met with the delicious smell of roasting meat and vegetables. Mrs. McCarthy stood at the counter with a bottle opener in hand—her blonde hair pulled back into a ponytail and a black and white patterned apron tied around her waist.

She looked over her shoulder and gave us a weak smile. "Hi, young lady."

"Hi, Mom."

"Owen, thank you for coming."

I took in a deep breath, my shoulders lifted slightly toward my ears. "Thank you for having me."

"It smells good. Roast beef?" Em nodded toward the oven.

"It sounded good. It's been so cold." Then Mrs. McCarthy's eyes went large and round. "You aren't vegetarian, right? I'm sure I could whip something else up for you. I didn't even think about it."

"Oh no, I-I'm good... I eat meat."

She ran a nervous hand down her cheek and cupped her neck. Guilt twisted in my gut. This lie was not fair to her or Mr. McCarthy.

"Oh gosh, you aren't picking on me. Things must be more strained than I thought," she said to Emmeline with a tense smile.

"Uh, I guess I'm just really sorry." There was a tightness to her words, as if they were being squeezed thin by a knot in her throat.

I reached my arm around her hunched shoulders, and she leaned into my side.

Her mom watched us for a moment before she took a step closer. Cupping Em's cheeks, she went up on her tiptoes and placed a kiss on her forehead. "I know. We're gonna move forward."

"How?"

I couldn't watch. Instead, I watched the way the light caught on icicles hanging just outside the kitchen window.

Mrs. McCarthy took a step back to lean against the counter, putting herself back in my line of vision. "I was talking to your aunt Lucy, she pointed out that we could meet Owen like we did anyone else you've dated. That you're a great judge of character." She shrugged. "That we didn't have to let this... That whatever caused all this secrecy doesn't have to be what matters."

Em squeezed tight to my side.

Her mom shook her hands as if wiping a chalkboard clean. "Anyway. Wine anyone?"

"Yes, please."

I shook my head. "I'm driving."

We helped set the table. Roast beef and vegetables steamed inside colorful bowls. Meeting a partner's parents was never a favorite of mine—the answering of questions, the attention. It wasn't a natural state for me. But much like her daughter, Mrs. McCarthy had a way of moving a conversation. There were few lulls and those were fairly comfortable.

"You two met at that little running group, right?" she asked before taking a bite.

I nodded.

"She talked to you right away, didn't she?"

A blush crept up Emmeline's face as her eyes widened. "*Mom.*"

"You're very handsome, Owen."

At her side, Mr. McCarthy's shoulders bounced.

"Thank you, Mrs. McCarthy." I laughed.

"Call me Vivian."

"*Okay*, Mom." Em had her face partially shielded behind her hand.

"Why are you so embarrassed?" Vivian asked.

"Well, she did talk to me right away," I answered. "Hardly even had my shoes tied."

Emmeline's mouth hung wide with indignation as she looked back at me, her hand thudding against the tabletop. "That's so unfair. So, you're telling me you wouldn't have talked to me?"

"I definitely would've. I noticed you before you even noticed me."

"How do you know that?"

"I saw you in the parking lot. I was in my truck, thinking about not joining the group, but then I saw you."

A brilliant smile split across her face. "But you weren't gonna talk to me."

"I was... eventually."

"But not as quickly as me."

"I'm shy." I shot her a crooked smile as I said it, hoping it sounded like a joke, even though it was true.

"He's shy, too." Vivian nudged her husband with her shoulder. "I had to talk to him first, too."

Mr. McCarthy nodded.

"He was a maintenance worker on campus. I kept seeing him, but he was mowing lawns or I was on my way to class." Her expression turned nostalgic. "But then, he was waiting in line for ice cream. I was so excited to finally get to talk to him that I didn't even notice he was on a date."

"You never told me that," Emmeline exclaimed.

"Not one of my finer moments."

"What'd you do?"

"I don't remember."

"You don't?" Mr. McCarthy smirked at his wife, clearly he knew she was lying. "She gave me a napkin with her number on it and said, 'If you ever wanna mow my lawn...'"

I half-choked on a carrot.

"Mother! Dad, that worked?!"

He scoffed, "Yeah."

"Oh my god! Mom, you were a booty call?"

She held up a manicured finger. "No, your dad was a booty call. I gave him my number, but I never intended to fall in love."

"Wow."

"I'm sure other love stories have stranger beginnings."

Em and I shared a glance, and whatever division had been between us wasn't there in that moment.

"How did I not know?"

"I guess we all have secrets sometimes."

"I wanna clarify. I just said, 'Hi, my name's Emmeline.'"

Vivian shrugged. "I guess that worked, too. Tell us about your parents, what do they do?"

"My dad worked for GM, and retired early when they offered the buyout in '08. My mom just retired from the FBI last year." I never knew whether to point out the complicated history between Hawaii and the military or how to tell people my mom's former profession—it always got attention.

Mr. McCarthy grunted, and Vivian's mouth fell open. At my side, Em blinked and I wondered if I'd ever told her.

"Wow. How long did she work there?" Vivian asked.

"A little over thirty years. It was the main reason dad moved here instead of them living in Hawaii. She was offered the job right around the time they met."

"How'd they meet?"

"She was in the army at the time, and she was discharged. After a couple of weeks of sending letters, Dad decided to give Michigan a try."

Vivian gave her husband an assessing look. "I don't know if I would give up Hawaii for you."

After our laughter quieted, Mr. McCarthy said, "I would."

The way Vivian fought the smile growing on her face reminded me so much of Emmeline that I couldn't resist reaching over and taking Em's hand. I'd grown familiar to the feel of her fingers, and the way her grip fit in mine.

She ran her thumb along the back of my knuckles. "Do they still have their letters?"

I nodded. "I've never read them, though. I'm sure there's things there, I don't want to know."

"What about you two? When did you fall in love?" Vivian lifted her fork to her mouth.

Em's chest lifted with a breath. "Uh…"

I didn't know what Em would have said next because I started talking—even though I'd already spoken more than I usually did. "It was quick for me. I didn't even realize it at the time, but it was the last group run. It was snowing, and you looked up and smiled at the sky, and when you looked back at me, there were snowflakes on your eyelashes." I swallowed, remembering the impact of that moment.

She blinked. "That was, like, last February."

"I know."

"Why didn't you say something?"

"You were dating that engineer."

"Oh right. But then we broke up in like, March."

We needed to be careful with our timeline.

"I didn't want to be a rebound, so I gave you time. And I don't know… I didn't want to start something when you needed a friend."

"When did you two start dating?" Mr. McCarthy asked.

"October," she nearly whispered.

"So this isn't as sudden for you as it is for us," Vivian pointed out.

I shook my head. "No, I feel like it's taken a long time."

# CHAPTER 17

## OWEN

Giant white flakes glowed in the headlights of my SUV on the way home, making the drive take twice as long.

We were silent the whole way home, but she held my hand, the smooth metal of her ring pressed against my fingers. I wanted to ask what she was thinking. I kept replaying the story I told about falling in love with her. It was the first time I'd realized the depth of my infatuation. The memory felt bright like a heartbeat on a sonogram.

A blip of light I'd never forget.

Sharing it had seemed the best way to sell our romance, to complete our con. But in the end, it revealed something I hadn't realized before.

That I've been in love with Emmeline for just shy of a year.

Was she reliving it, too? Was she wondering what it meant? Did she know it was real?

Did she feel the same way?

We were still quiet when we let the dogs out and got ready for bed. I generally associated Emmeline with energy and conversation, but I'd realized she grew quiet when she puzzled through something. I should say something—ask what was on her mind—but I couldn't bring myself to.

After brushing my teeth, I stepped out of the bathroom and found her sitting on the edge of the bed. Her baggy sweatshirt hung off one shoulder. She looked up at me when I stood in front of her, her ocean-colored eyes full of... I didn't know what.

The skin of her shoulder was soft under my palm. I trailed my fingers up her neck to run my thumb over her parted lips. Her sigh traveled up my wrist. Pale eyelashes rested against pink skin.

I bent to place a kiss on her forehead, and she sat straighter and leaned closer. She grabbed my sides as if she were holding on to me for support. Our noses nuzzled and our lips met.

My heart stopped for just a moment.

A quick stutter at the barest contact.

Her gasp told me she had felt it, too.

"Em..."

My vision was filled with aqua blue, her black pupils large.

"Owen," she whispered. All the vulnerability and hesitation I was feeling was right there, in my name on her lips. She leaned that perfect mouth toward me and closed the gap. A test, a gentle sweep. Dipping my toe in the water, only to realize it was a pool I never wanted to surface from.

"I love you," she breathed.

I felt her words against my skin just as much as I felt them inside. I smiled as my mouth landed on hers. I wrapped my arms around her back and pressed her tight to me, half picking her up off the bed. Her hands hooked around my shoulders and her legs wrapped around my waist.

But her mouth discovered mine as earnestly as I discovered hers. Searching, biting, needing to taste deeper, to linger longer. I would give up breathing if it meant kissing her until I died.

I half laid down, half fell on the bed. I rolled onto my back, bringing her with me. We didn't stop kissing. She tasted of toothpaste and passion, and I couldn't get enough.

She held me, completely wrapped around me as if I might disappear.

But I wasn't going anywhere.

I'd built a dam on the flow of my feelings, allowing only the smallest trickle to seep through, but the dam was obliterated. And I was overwhelmed by everything I'd pushed back. I clung to her like a safety-line.

The fabric of her shirt was soft against the backs of my hands as they traveled up the firm plane of her stomach to cup her breast in my palm, and she arched her back.

We broke our kiss for just a moment to push her shirt over her head.

I shifted her underneath me, pressing her back into the mattress under my weight.

She shivered as my lips followed the line of her neck. Her breaths shuddered at the flick of my tongue against her stiff nipple. Her fingers trailed from my hair all the way down my spine. My body recognized something in her, something that made every touch and sigh, every scent and quiver feel like they happened in an echo. Her pleasure was my pleasure.

Fulfilling her needs fulfilled mine.

I was hers.

"Owen, please," she gasped. "I need you."

I looked up. A glistening line drew down her temple and disappeared into her hair.

I cradled her face. "What's wrong?"

"Nothing." She shook her head. "Please, I just need you. I need you inside me."

She pushed her shorts down her legs. I stood to take off my shirt and shorts. Turning to grab a condom, I stopped when she said, "I'm on the pill, and I tested negative for STIs."

I turned back to look at her. "I don't have anything, either."

Her arms were wrapped around her knees, hugging them to her chest.

Considering her, I asked. "Are you okay?"

"I'm okay. It just got intense for a minute, you know."

"We don't have to have sex. I can just hold you."

"Do you not want to?"

I looked down at my almost painful erection and raised an eyebrow at her. "Oh, I want to."

Again, she met my gaze.

Again, I couldn't identify the emotion there.

It was too sad to be love. It carved out my chest.

I knelt on the bed and met her in the middle. Her legs slid out on the bed. I wanted to pick up where we'd left off, but something wasn't right. I laid on my side next to her, drawing my fingertips up and down her arm. There was something I was missing in the past couple of minutes, I was sure of it. Something that would make her sad eyes make sense.

"Why are you just lying there?"

"I'm thinking," I answered.

"I don't think we need to think right now—"

My "oh" interrupted her when I realized what I'd messed up. I rolled and braced myself on my fists on either side of her shoulders.

"I love you, too." I spoke with all the conviction I felt. I didn't know if I'd ever meant anything as much as I meant those words.

The unease between her brows disappeared. "Y-you do?"

"I love you so much, Emmeline."

"It's just... you didn't say anything..."

"I know, and I'm sorry."

"And it was okay if you didn't, I just really wanted you to—"

"I do."

Lowering, I laid on top of her. Our kisses were slower and more tender. She spread her legs to welcome me, and I eased my cock at her entrance. She shifted until I was completely seated inside of her, hot and wet.

Our stomachs pressed together as we kissed and fucked with easy gentleness.

Her ankles crossed behind my back as she tightened around me; until she squeezed so earth-shatteringly tight that I couldn't take it much longer. Her jaw fell open in a silent scream as her walls spasmed. I pressed my forehead to her shoulder and dug my fingers into her hips as I came. I was still catching my breath when I turned my head to look at her. A tear slipped down her temple.

"Em." My voice was a hoarse whisper against her neck.

She shivered.

We laid on our sides, her leg hooked over my waist with my arm under her head. It was going to cut off circulation, but she looked too comfortable for me to move it. I was nearly asleep and too satisfied to care.

# CHAPTER 18

## EMMELINE

The morning after telling my fake-husband I was in love with him didn't go as planned—not that there was a plan but waking up late and frantic definitely hadn't been it. We passed out the night before, naked and spent without setting alarms. He had to skip his jog with Bandit, who complained loudly and bullied Venice in the backyard. The other dog yipped and played, completely oblivious to Bandit's bad mood.

Starting my day late would normally not be an issue at all—I typically didn't have to go into the office, but I was scheduled to ride along with Sam to see some of my former clients—just a couple of accounts whose sales could improve. We'd done one a few months ago, and I'd filled the silence by talking about *anything* as we drove from location to location. Silent men were a standard in my life, but Sam brought it to a whole new level.

Owen and I hardly even kissed goodbye as we dashed to our cars. My mouth hung open, wondering if I should tell him again that I loved him. The words were right there—had been since I'd told him the night before, but no words came out.

"I..." he started, then shook his head. "Have a good day."

"You, too," I said brightly, though my stomach twisted, wondering why I didn't repeat how I felt. But it was too late now, he was backing out of the driveway.

This was what I had been afraid of. The state of our relationship—or whatever it was—was too tender. In the light of day, we weren't as bold as when we were wrapped around each other. It was going to fall apart. He'd even acknowledged it when he asked, *How are we going to end this?*

Even with those words touring through my head the day before, I'd told him I loved him, and I regretted not telling him again this morning.

Maybe there was a way for it to work.

With my hair pinned poorly into a French twist and only having time to apply mascara, I walked into the office I shared with Sam five minutes late. The off-white walls were empty of decorations. On my desk, I had a photo of a Lake Michigan sunset—I was careful not to show signs of having a life outside of work. People often questioned my commitment. What would happen if I got married and had a family? Would I still give my clients the attention they were used to? It was best just to avoid the conversation all together—of course, until I had told everyone I was married. So far, I hadn't had to field those questions, but I was ready for them, anyway.

Sam sat at his desk with his back to me—his posture perfect. A photo of his niece and nephew were placed where anyone could see it next to his monitor.

How quickly could I tell him we needed to hit a coffee shop for politeness' sake? Did it have to be after the first meeting? Could I say it right now?

"Good morning."

He looked over his shoulder. "Hi."

"Sorry I'm late."

"No worries, just getting some paperwork done. Thanks for making time to help me out."

"Of course." I set my bag on my desk, then picked it back up. "I'm sorry. I need coffee."

Somehow his perfect posture straightened. "Okay, uh... I can finish this later."

I slumped into my chair. "No, I can wait."

"Late night?"

I shrugged. "Kinda."

My phone buzzed inside my bag. I had to do some digging to get it out, but when I read the text from Owen, a smile split across my face.

*I love you. I should have told you back home. This drive to work sucked. I just wanna be with you.*

*I love you, too,* I replied. *I wanted to say it, too. I don't know why I didn't.*

"Your husband?" Sam asked.

My stomach flipped, but this time not because of the lie. Instead, it was the insinuation that Owen was *mine*.

I looked away from the three little dots to my coworker. The smallest smile twinkled in his eyes.

"Yeah."

"That's beautiful."

"What is?"

"The way you lit up when you got that text. That's love. It's beautiful."

A blush warmed my cheeks, and I grinned down at the floor. Love bloomed like wildflowers in my chest. My phone buzzed again, but I'd have to read it in the car. It would be too rude to continue chatting with Owen when I'd pretty much forced Sam to stop working.

"I still need that coffee." I nodded toward the office door.

"Lead the way. Is it okay if I drive?"

"I'd prefer it."

***

Sam had been downright chatty. He opened up about his move from Indiana to Michigan for this job, and how he was struggling to find a community.

"You've probably noticed, but I'm pretty quiet," he muttered on our drive back to the office.

"Couldn't tell."

"Yeah, I bet you couldn't."

"What does that mean?"

His mouth hung open, staring out the windshield as if his brain had gone offline. "Uh... I-I didn't know you were seeing anyone. I'm not a creep—which I'm sure is what creeps say, but I'm not. So, I'm not social..."

I remained silent to give him room to explain.

"And it gets worse around people I'm attracted to, and you're my boss' daughter and really nice and very good at your job." He swallowed. "Again, I didn't know you were seeing anyone. I had you built up too much in my head, so I couldn't talk around you."

"But since I'm married, you're good now?"

His smile was more of a cringe. "Yeah."

"Dating must be fun."

"I'm gonna die alone." He smiled his winsome smile.

I shared with him that I was struggling to connect with Micheals, leaving out the discrimination in the retelling and my lie about my relationship with Owen.

"He sounds... like a challenge."

I barked a laugh.

"Just do your job; he's never going to be friendly."

"I don't even know what my job looks like if I'm not friendly with my clients."

"Because you're a woman."

My stomach dropped. I had really thought we were bonding. "What?"

"You have to try harder. I can say three words in a visit, and I look like the strong, silent type."

I nodded, understanding his meaning.

"Put your attention on other clients." He reiterated my thoughts.

It kind of felt like defeat, though.

He shifted in his seat. "It sounds like you'll work your ass off for that guy and it'll never be enough."

I chewed on my lower lip. "If I tell you something, do you promise not to tell anyone."

"I actively try not to speak to people as much as possible, so yeah, I promise."

I laughed again. "That's why Owen and I announced our marriage. We weren't going to yet, but then Micheals said he wouldn't work with an unmarried woman, and I panicked." I paused to breathe through the remembered anxiety sparking in my body. The way Micheals spoke as if everything he was saying was proper; the way Meridith, his business administrator, looked anywhere but at me.

"That's... that's unacceptable." Sam's mouth hung open.

There was relief in telling him even that much of the truth.

By the time I got home that evening, I buzzed with the electricity of making a new friend. It really felt like I had.

I grabbed a snack after letting the dogs out—Bandit was still in a shitty mood. I was going to take him for a jog, but when I sat in the recliner to put on my shoes, Maui jumped off the sofa. Ella and I both looked up in confusion as he trotted the short distance to hop onto my lap.

Sitting back, I stared down at the little dog. He laid down in the seam where my thighs pressed together.

That was how Owen found us the almost an hour later.

"Holy shit," he said in welcome.

I held my phone in one hand, reading an eBook, while my other rested on Maui's head. My thumb stroked behind his ear. "I am just as surprised as you."

His scrubs fit his frame like fabric boxes, yet the sight of him made my heart skip a beat.

Owen blinked between me and his dog. "How did it happen?"

"He just came over and sat down."

"Wow." The most dazzling smile split his lips and that delicious dimple pressed into his cheek. "Woman, you are magical."

I bit my lower lip, but it didn't keep my smile from spreading.

Hooking his finger under my chin, Owen guided me to look up at him. His lips were warm and soft on mine. My toes curled in my socks. Time slowed, stretching this moment a few breaths longer.

He pulled away just far enough to press his forehead to mine. "I've wanted to do that all day."

I sighed. "Me, too."

Maui growled low.

"Oh, I'm sorry." Owen smirked down at the little dog. "Did I disturb you?"

His knuckle stroked down the column of my neck to the neckline of my long-sleeve T-shirt. It followed the fabric to the tops of my breasts, and my nipples stiffened. He kissed me again, but this time it was urgent, full of need.

My breaths were shallow when he stepped back and lowered himself to the armrest. He ran his fingers through Ella's long fur. "How was your day?"

I had to blink, recalling the purpose of language. "Uh, great! I had that ride-along with Sam, and he actually talked to me the entire time. It was nice. I actually told him a bit about that nightmare client and talked it out with him. He's actually like, really funny and pleasant."

"Huh. He's usually quiet, right?" Owen lowered his head, making it impossible for me to see his face.

"So quiet... like quieter than you."

"What changed?"

"He said he's really shy and has a hard time talking to people he likes, but since I'm not on the market, he was able to talk to me."

Owen's nodded. "So, he likes you."

"Um, I guess he *did* but not anymore."

"You're married, and all of a sudden that goes away?"

There was an edge to Owen's voice that prickled at my skin. "I don't know. I'm not responsible for his feelings."

"No." He shook his head like it needed clearing. His fingers trailed through his silky black hair. "I'm glad you had a good day. I'm gonna take Bandit for a run."

"Okay."

"Do you want anything to drink or something?" He gestured toward Maui. "Clearly, you're never getting up again."

"Yeah, this is where I live now. Water would be great."

He stood over me, his feet shoulder-width apart. His hand cupped my throat, his thumb under my chin. With a primal heat in his eyes, he looked down at me. His fingers were placed right over my pulse, so he must have felt how it skipped. "You're so fucking beautiful."

I turned to liquid under the heat of his stare. "If you're going to get that run done, you better leave now, or I won't let you go anywhere."

A muscle jumped in his jaw. He looked like he was debating whether he had to go, but then Bandit let out a howl of protest.

"Why do I have so many fucking dogs?" he groaned.

I giggled and watched as he walked to the kitchen.

But my fear from earlier returned. This couldn't last when it was weighed down so heavily. It was too brittle a of connection. I wanted to be wrong, but it felt like it would break. And when—*if*—it broke, it would be jagged.

I couldn't see how I would heal correctly.

But Sam had seen how much I loved Owen, and Owen had to see it, too. I could believe in this string that tied the two of us together. I could believe it was made of something stronger, a material that could improve under the strain of deception.

# CHAPTER 19

## OWEN

Stepping out of the shower with my hair still dripping and a towel wrapped around my waist, I was struck with the sight of Emmeline bent over, rubbing lotion on her bare legs in our bedroom. Looking at her, with her hair in a sloppy bun atop her head and a worn T-shirt hanging just past her bare ass, it was obvious why anyone would be interested in her. She was striking. The sharp, strong lines of her body balanced with the bright warmth that filled her eyes.

It wasn't Sam wanting her that made me feel like I'd been thrown into a lion's den naked; it was the opening of a hurt I had never really healed from. Emmeline said she loved me, but so had Natalie. But Natalie had broken my heart to be with the friend she told me not to worry about. And she consistently said one thing but meant another.

And Emmeline had liked Sam before... all of this.

My second-guessing was sickeningly familiar.

What if she decided she wanted him more than she wanted me?

That possibility shattered me into a million little pieces. This felt real, but so did my fear. Angst sank deep, like marrow in my bones, that in a couple of days she would slip away from me.

I stood behind her, not giving a shit about the wet footprints on the hardwood floors. My skin needed hers.

I slipped my arm around her ribs. Her hands were slick with lotion as they gripped my forearm pressed between her breasts underneath her shirt. I gripped where her shoulder met her neck, and I half bent to her, half pulled her up to meet me. She could probably feel my heart's panicked beating between her shoulder blades.

Her head fell back against my shoulder as a moan rumbled in her throat.

My other hand raked down her stomach, which flexed under my palm. She gasped as I cupped between her naked thighs, the hair atop her mound simultaneously soft and coarse against my palm. She arched into my touch, her back pressed against my chest.

Gently, I found her dampness with my middle finger. I craved to be inside her, but I wouldn't give into it until she was ready for me.

The terry cloth of the towel rubbed against my hard cock as she shifted her hips to allow my finger to ease in and out.

I drew my teeth along the skin of her shoulder, careful not to bite too hard.

Whatever was feral within me was met by the same animal in her. She reached her hand between us, loosening the knot of the towel, which slipped to the floor. She gripped my length, slipping her hand from my base to tip and back again.

I felt her touch in my spine.

The first time we'd fucked, I'd needed it to happen again. Cataloging everything she seemed to like best, the places she preferred to be touched. I'd learned so much about her body since then. I knew how to make her come, I knew how to draw it out, and she knew the same for me.

But the sick fear that all this was temporary formed a torturous pit in my stomach. No matter how much I tried to calm it, I couldn't.

I whispered next to her ear, "Slip the head of my cock along your cunt."

My finger slipped from her warmth. She went up on her tiptoes and eased me along her slit. Her soft heat felt so familiar, and I ached to sink inside her. The back and forth was slow, so different than the urgency coursing through me.

I guided her to look over her shoulder. When her lust-soaked eyes were locked onto mine, I lifted my finger, glistening from her wetness, and sucked it between my lips. Her walls flexed around the head of my cock as her slick wetness dripped down my length. She'd be so tight around me.

Her free hand hooked backward and pulled my mouth to hers. The flavor of her cunt and her mouth mingled and made my hair stand on end.

She pressed her hips back, but I pulled away, keeping my tip at her entrance and no deeper.

A protest whimpered from her throat.

I jerked my head toward the bed. "Kneel on the bed."

Her breathing was shallow as she complied.

"Ass up."

The T-shirt inched to the middle of her waist, and I took in the sight of her, her face pressed against the comforter, watching me savor her. Her clit was swollen, the lips of her pussy glistened.

I ran my hand possessively over her round ass, then trailed a finger down the seam. She puckered at my barest touch. I drew my finger down where she was drenched, to circle and tease her nub. An addictive moan had me withdraw my finger to repeat the process. My cock twitched. I was so hard it hurt.

After the third circuit, she groaned, "Please, Owen."

"Can you tell me what you want?" I'd give her anything.

"Isn't it clear what I want?"

"Is it?"

"I want you inside me." It was a near whisper. My bold Emmeline struggled to find her voice in our bed.

The tip of my cock found her entrance. My hand rested at the base of her spine as I eased into her. Her hips lifted and she gasped into the mattress as I buried myself completely. She moved, pulling me in and pushing me out.

Did she need me like I needed her? Would she have me? Would she have all of me, always?

I slid my arms around her ribs and pulled her against my chest. She gripped my hair at the base of my neck and her mouth found mine. She whimpered when my hand drifted to her sensitive clit.

The back of her head fell onto my shoulder. I ran my teeth and tongue along her neck to her ear. My mind went blank except for the sensation of her squeezing me tighter and tighter. The way her breath caught and held as she neared her orgasm.

"Emmeline," I whispered against her skin. "Emmeline. Emmeline."

There was nothing but her. There was nothing but this.

Neither of us cried out as we came. Our bodies had taken every sip of oxygen and given it up. My vision turned dark as her walls spasmed around me and I spilled inside her. We fell forward on the bed, gasping.

She breathed quick, shallow breaths in my arms. Her heart pounded against my forearm. I kissed her shoulder where my teeth had marked her and ran my hand down her hip and up her side. Her breathing leveled and slowed with each inhale and exhale.

My arms had never held something so tightly, with so much fear of losing it.

Losing her.

Or worse, that she was never really mine in the first place.

***

The next day was a study in going through the motions until I got home. My days had felt more and more like that lately—time spent away from Em was less time spent with her. She sat on the recliner she'd brought over with her laptop open on her lap. Her skirt was bunched up around her mid-thighs, and her skin looked so smooth I could almost feel it. On the screen, Laurie smiled a hello to me when I came into view.

"Hi." I waved before bending to kiss Em. It didn't matter that Laurie knew the truth, because for me, kissing Emmeline had never been for show. "I'm gonna take Bandit for a run."

"Okay, have fun."

"Good to see you, Owen," Laurie said.

"You, too."

When I got back, Emmeline was closing her computer. "I'll take Bandit out tomorrow when I get home so we can just head out to the restaurant when you get home."

"Sounds good." I picked up the hem of my T-shirt and wiped my face, enjoying the way she looked at my exposed skin.

She chewed her lower lip for a moment. "What got into you last night?"

"What do you mean?"

"Um… It was great, just like… intense."

I swallowed. I should tell her; she deserved to know. But the feeling that a crowded room of eyes stared at me kept the words locked inside. I hated talking about my breakup with Natalie. It was years ago, and we were young. It shouldn't keep me from connecting with other people, but it did.

Emmeline stood and took my hand. "Are you okay?"

"Yeah, why?"

"You just look like maybe you're not."

With my free hand, I pinched the bridge of my nose. "I'm okay."

Sighing, I said, "My ex, Natalie, dumped me to be with the guy she told me not to worry about. So yesterday, when you were talking about Sam, I got… jealous." I met her concerned gaze. "This is my problem, Em. I know that."

She nodded in understanding. "I'm not into Sam."

I swallowed. I wanted to believe her, but just a few weeks ago she'd been talking about how she wanted to get dinner with him.

Sliding my arms around her back, I pulled her against my chest, and she automatically rested her head on my shoulder.

"Thanks for telling me," she said.

I nodded. She felt so right in my arms.

"We still don't have a plan for how we end this," she whispered into my neck.

I pulled back to meet her eyes. The way she said, *'end this,'* had recalled my thoughts from a couple of days before, and made me wonder if there was more she wasn't saying.

I didn't have an answer, and I didn't want to think about letting her go. "Wanna figure it out later?"

"Sure."

I tilted my head, her lips touched mine, and I sank into her taste and warmth. But I still felt a lingering doubt that the relationship growing between us couldn't be trusted. I wanted to believe that she wouldn't find someone she wanted more than me. At least I could ignore it while I kissed her.

# Chapter 20

## Emmeline

Owen put his SUV into park outside the restaurant. His grip was tight around the steering wheel.

My thumb tapped a quick beat on my knee. We still hadn't made a plan for ending this... arrangement. We were in limbo, and I hated being in limbo. Waiting was challenging, it took patience, and in this case, I didn't know what I was waiting for. We told each other how we felt, we lived together comfortably, but what did that mean? Were we in a long-term relationship?

I hadn't found anything I wanted to cut and run from yet.

His weirdness about Sam might have been enough, but then Owen was honest about why he felt that way.

I needed to move home, right? We couldn't keep this up, right? And when I did move back home, what would that mean? Would we start dating? Everyone we knew would be so confused. Who dates their ex-husband in the same week of their separation?

We could say we were working on it...

I couldn't go back to just being his friend after all this. Not with the way I loved him.

Even with the stakes stacked against us, it didn't feel like a lost cause.

Shifting his back against the driver's side door, his hazel eyes roamed my face, as if memorizing me. He drew his thumb down my cheek. "Hey, there."

I sighed and smiled. "Hi."

Maybe all my trepidation was for nothing. We would find a way for it to work.

I leaned across the center counsel and pressed a chaste kiss to his lips. Jerking my head toward the front door of the restaurant, I asked, "You ready?"

He nodded.

"You nervous?"

"Why would I be nervous?"

"I don't know. People."

He snorted. "No, I'm good."

We held hands as we hurried across the parking lot. It was early evening, but the sky was dark and full of heavy clouds blocking out the stars.

Inside, buffet tables were set up along one wall, silver stands waiting for their dishes. A large portion of the people in attendance were my coworkers and their spouses. It was supposed to be a customer appreciation dinner, but every year it was mostly employees.

The circular tables were covered in maroon and black, matching our company colors. Little laminated signs sat in the center of the tables on silver stands, thanking different businesses for their patronage.

I scanned the crowd and found Sam sitting alone, looking at his phone. My coat pocket vibrated. On my watch, both Owen and I glance down to read the text from Sam.

***You still coming or should I bail? This is my nightmare.***

"Come on, let's go save him from himself." I smirked at Owen, but something passed behind his eyes. Clearly, my reassurance the night before hadn't scrubbed all his insecurities away. I bit my lip and told myself it wasn't a big deal. He'd admitted that it was his problem. He'd work on it.

It'd be okay.

But a queasy feeling slithered in my belly.

"We have come to save the day," I joked, taking a seat at Sam's table.

He sighed and some of the tension released from his shoulders. "Day saved." Standing, he held out a hand. "Owen, good to see you again."

Owen accepted it, then lowered into the seat next to me and draped his arm over my shoulders. "Good to see you, too."

Why couldn't he see how wrong he was about me and Sam? I should have explained that even when I was trying to shift my interest onto Sam, it didn't work—because the person I always wanted was Owen. There was no reason for him to feel threatened.

When we went home tonight, we would talk. We'd make an actual plan for ending our lie but find a way to stay together. We had a lot to overcome, and I wanted to believe we could do it.

*It'll be okay.* I wiped my sweaty palms on my slacks.

His jaw was a bit tight, and his voice sounded slightly monotone as he said, "How are your accounts doing? Em said you had a good ride-along the other day."

Sam nodded at his clasped hands. "Yeah, it was a big help."

"Good."

A thick, awkward silence settled at the table. Owen looked past us at the crowd, a crease between his eyebrows. Sam continued to watch his hands as if they had a habit of leaping off his wrists. I perused my mind of every detail I knew about both of them, searching for some common ground. It was slim pickings. They were both introverts to the next degree, and that was about it.

"Hey, did you know that my uncle Dutch had tried to get both of you to date my cousin Laurie? So, if you thought you were special there, you're not." I sounded too chipper and my voice was too loud, but I'd found something for them to bond over.

Sam blinked up at me. "That must have been awkward."

"You know first-hand how awkward it is."

"Was it while you were dating?"

My cheeks warmed and reflexively, I looked at Owen.

He sat motionless.

"Yeah, but you know, no one knew…" I hoped the explanation would be enough.

The faintest smirk lifted Sam's lips. "Lucky you got married. I haven't found a way for it to stop yet."

Relief rushed through me.

"He's persistent." Owen grimaced.

Was I imagining the tinge of regret in his voice?

"I swear, Laurie has nothing to do with any of this. She hasn't found a way for it to end, either." My voice was light and easy, even though my stomach knotted.

Something was wrong and it was getting worse. I could feel it growing, but this wasn't the time for me to fix it. Owen was sitting right next to me, but he was so far away.

"Maybe you should get her number," Owen suggested to Sam. "Giving in might be the only solution."

"She would not be impressed." I shook my head, thinking about the hellfire she'd give poor Sam.

He chuckled. "Can you imagine a more awkward beginning to a relationship?"

Owen made a "hmm" sound that made my skin feel tight.

"I'm awkward enough; we don't need to add that on top of it." Sam smirked.

"You're not awkward," I argued.

He lifted a light brown eyebrow.

"Okay, you are, but once you get past that, you're a total catch." I shot him goofy finger guns. "A bona fide beau-hunk."

"What an endorsement." He smiled his full, fetching smile.

At my side, Owen went even stiffer.

"I think I'm going to get a water, you two want anything?" His arm slipped from my shoulders, and I wished I could get the weight of it back. If I'd felt like there was distance growing before, it was immense now.

I wanted to tell him that whatever was going through his mind was wrong; that whatever he thought he saw between Sam and me wasn't real.

Instead, I replied, "White wine, please."

Lifting a water glass sweating on the table, Sam said, "Thanks though."

Owen rolled his head from one shoulder to the other, stretching his neck as he walked away.

I forced my face to remain neutral. Under the table, my thumb tapped against my knee.

"Are you tight with your cousin?" Sam asked.

The table next to us grew loud, and I had to lean in close to hear him.

"Yeah, my family is kinda small and tight-knit. Laurie and I are only a couple of months apart."

"My family is huge." He shook his head. "So loud."

"Oh, we're a loud bunch, too."

"Your dad's kinda quiet, though, right?"

I shrugged. "He is, but the rest of us are obnoxious."

"So, you fit right in."

My eyes widened and my jaw dropped. "Really? Wow."

His cheeks reddened. "I'm joking."

"Oh my god, I know." I laughed and squeezed his shoulder in reassurance.

"Mrs. McCarthy," a voice I recognized said from behind me.

I took the smallest moment to gather myself—a deep breath to calm the spike of anger in my chest—before I stood and turned with a pleasant smile plastered on my face.

"Mr. Micheals, it's a pleasure to see you. I didn't realize you'd be here this evening."

"I don't normally attend events with alcohol, but I hoped I might get to meet your husband." He extended a hand to Sam. "Spencer Micheals."

He stood and took the offered hand. "Sam Hutchinson."

Owen arrived with a wineglass in one hand and a glass of ice water in the other. The set of his shoulders was even tighter than they were before he left. They looked like they wanted to press against his ears, and he had to actively force them down.

I took my drink, but he didn't meet my eye.

"Thank you. Mr. Micheals, this is my husband, Owen Kauahi."

Micheals blinked confusedly between Sam and Owen. "Oh, this is your husband?"

Owen and I shared a glance.

"I assumed you were sitting with your husband."

A muscle jumped in Owen's jaw.

"He was just grabbing drinks." I held up the glass in my hand as proof.

Micheals made a sound of disapproval, and I felt my face heat. The night was young, but I'd already had enough of it. First there was the tension between me and Owen, and now this near-stranger had the audacity to be condescending about my beverage choices.

But then, I'd misplaced so much of my power in this partnership.

I was done.

The litany of accusations on the tip of my tongue were hard to swallow, but instead, I said, "You know, I'm actually not feeling great. Owen, do you mind if we head home early?"

He nodded.

Micheals' bushy eyebrows drew together.

"I hope you have a lovely night," I said to him, but any idiot would be able to tell that I didn't mean it at all. Bending, I set my drink on the table and grabbed my coat off the back of my seat.

Sam placed a hand atop mine. "Are you okay?"

I nodded. "See ya Monday."

"Sure."

Owen turned on his heels and weaved toward the door. I followed him, but was slowed by hellos from various coworkers and clients. By the time I caught up to him, he was halfway across the parking lot.

My mood had shifted from sympathetic of his insecurities to fed-up. Whatever had him acting like such an asshole was beyond the tiny thread of patience I had left. "Owen, can you stop running away from me?"

He looked over his shoulder. "You said you wanted to leave."

"Yeah, but like, together, not with me jogging after you in heels on an ice-covered parking lot."

His sigh came out as a puff of steam illuminated by the lamppost above, but he took a step closer to me. "Why are you wearing such ridiculous shoes?"

"They go with my outfit. And I didn't know I'd be doing sprints on the way home. What is going on here?"

Stuffing his hands into his coat pockets, he looked down at the asphalt. "What was that, Em?"

"You'll have to be more specific. I honestly don't know what your problem is."

"I told you about my past."

"I understand your insecurities, but I'm going to be friends with men."

"I know that."

I took the last few strides to close the distance between us. "Then what is this?"

"You and Sam have gotten pretty friendly, pretty fast."

My jaw dropped and my eyes bulged.

His shoulders slumped, and he raked his fingers through his hair. "Look, I know I'm like this. I know I'm dealing with this shit. But it wasn't just *me*; that client of yours saw it, too. I saw his face when he found out you're married to *me*, not *Sam*."

I shook my head, and some of my outrage subsided. "Oh no. Owen, no. That's *the* client. That's the one who caused this whole mess. That's how condescending that guy is all the time. That's what I'm dealing with."

When he met my eyes, I recoiled at the betrayal I saw there. "I don't know, Em. You were into Sam before we... got together. It just seems too convenient that all of a sudden he's talking to you and you're whispering in his ear while I get your drink."

"I was not whispering in his ear. It was loud and we couldn't hear. I—" I looked around the dark parking lot and took a calming breath. "You have *nothing* to worry about, Owen. I'm not into Sam."

Owen rocked back on his heels as if I'd struck him. Obviously, I'd picked the wrong words.

"I'm *into* you." I reached out and squeezed his arm. "I've always been into you."

He stepped backward out of my grip. For a moment, my hand hung there between us until I let it fall back to my side.

"I don't know," he said. "That's the shitty thing... I don't know what to believe. I want to believe you, and I know I can't trust my instincts. And, okay, that client is an asshole, but he still saw what I saw. I left your side and Sam filled that space like I'd never been there. I don't know, I feel... replaceable." Owen scraped a hand over his throat, as if the word hurt him, as if it was tore through him like it did to me.

The vinegar coursing through my veins quieted. "No. No. You're anything but. I... Owen, I tried to replace you, but I couldn't."

"What?"

"I tried to like Sam, but I couldn't because I liked you."

He crossed his arms over his chest and took another step back. His eyes looked black in the dim light. "You *tried* to replace me with Sam?"

I shook my head and grimaced—everything was getting twisted. "Not like that."

"Like what, then?"

"Well, kinda like that, but before I knew how you felt about me."

"So, I was replaceable before?"

I pulled my coat closed tighter, but the cold felt like it was coming from the inside out. "No, stop it. You're not replaceable. Jesus, it's like you've been waiting years to have this fight. That Natalie girl did a number on you, and now you can't believe me when I tell you how I feel about you."

The crease between his eyebrows deepened. "Yeah, that's about it."

We stood like statues frozen in place. Reality sunk down on us with each breath—heavy and frigid.

"I think I should probably stay at my house tonight," I whispered, but it rang like a shout in my head.

He nodded.

"I think we got swept up, and things got confused. We should probably think about what all of this means," I said.

More nodding.

I wished he'd fight.

I wished I would too, but I didn't.

I looked up at the black sky just past the dome of lights. Something inside me knew this was the end I'd been dreading. My chest was too tight, each breath shallower than the one before it. I didn't know if I was shivering from the winter night or the way our fragile thread had been cut.

A bad break.

His boots crunched on the parking lot as he turned away from me and walked to his truck. "I'll take you to your car; I'm sure there's stuff at my house you need." He held the passenger door open.

I considered telling him to leave, even though I didn't want to go back inside the restaurant, and I didn't want to text any of my coworkers for a ride. This was the kind of drama that would blaze like wildfire.

And yes, there were essentials at his house, but I couldn't care less about them.

My heart was lead inside my ribcage. It was heavy and sore, and it might have made a wrong turn along the way, but it still wanted to be near Owen's.

So, I climbed into the open door and closed it behind me.

# Chapter 21

## Owen

I was covered in dog piss, and that seemed about right. It matched my mood.

Luckily, a soon-to-be divorced man wasn't expected to be cheery.

That first Monday after Em moved out, I'd arrived to work without my ring. If I hadn't reached to twirl it around—a habit I hadn't realized I'd developed until the ring was gone—most likely no one would have noticed.

"Oh no, did you lose your ring?" Mandi, the volunteer coordinator, asked.

"We're taking a break," I lied.

She gasped. "What happened?"

"I don't want to talk about it." At least that had been the truth.

I wanted to go back to when my work life and my personal life were separate.

Almost a week ago, Em had thrown stuff into a bag with the speed of someone fleeing the scene and had gone back to her house. I leaned against the kitchen counter and watched her taillights disappear. Each second carved me out until I was nothing but a shell.

My dogs still whined for her, and Maui was particularly irritable. I couldn't really blame him, and even though it was for the best, I was irritable, too.

I had been hopeful that things would have gone differently with Em—and it was the hope I still struggled with. We hadn't actually broken up, but we also hadn't spoken in five days. Break up or not, it felt done.

The rubber soles of my shoes scraped against the tile floor of the medical building as I went from the exam room to my office. I passed Molly's door without looking in her direction, but I knew she noticed me by the pause in her typing. When the beagle we were treating started peeing, she'd reached for the mop. I'd told her I would take care of it. Keeping busy was my main objective.

Slowing down meant thinking.

Thoughts were confusing.

Memories hurt.

But then I'd slipped on the piss, and that hurt, too.

I opened the little cabinet in my office, expecting to see a spare set of scrubs. Instead, there was nothing. Just empty hangers.

My teeth ground together.

"Hey, doc," Molly's tentative voice came from the open door to the hallway, "you okay?"

As gently as possible, I shut the door. "Yeah."

"Do you wanna talk?"

I shook my head. "I'm good. Do you have an extra set of scrubs?"

"I think so. I'll be right back."

Molly had a bright orange set. I looked like an escaped inmate.

***

"Bandit, heel." I jerked on his leash to give my command weight. It certainly wasn't in my voice.

He ignored me.

He wanted to run faster, but my fall earlier really did not feel good. I needed to take it easy. I'd been running harder and longer than usual over the past few days. Bandit was usually panting by the time we got home, and my heart felt like it would pound out of my chest. The tight soreness in my muscles felt good, like punishment or absolution. It was also why my slip had caused a slight limp in my stride.

"Bandit, heel. This is it, man, this is as good as it gets." I was talking about our jog, but my words struck my chest like arrows finding their mark.

Instead of investigating the feeling any further, I picked up my pace.

In the garage, I limped with my hands atop my head. My hair was damp with sweat, and my lungs demanded breath. Bandit sniffed the cement where Em's car used to park. I was still off to the side, as if she might need to take up that spot. It was a habit that I'd break, eventually—just like making a pot of coffee for two people in the morning instead of one. Just like rolling over in the middle of the night to find her side of the bed cold.

How had the rhythm with her been so strongly and effectively set in such a short amount of time?

He whined and yipped at me, as if we should go looking for our lost pack member.

"Come on, let's go inside," I said after my breathing leveled some.

Opening the door, four sets of eyes looked up at me. The dogs shared sighs before laying their heads back down between their paws. It'd be funny how synchronized the whole bit was if it wasn't so goddamn depressing.

"Hi, guys."

Venice's and Indie's tails thumped half-heartedly against the floor. Ella lifted concerned eyebrows. Maui growled.

I ignored him.

An hour later, I wrapped icepacks around both of my knees and my sore hip, when my phone buzzed. I didn't bother checking it. Remi had been hovering, which was impressive considering he was halfway across the country. He was convinced I should feel terrible, and he wasn't wrong. It would feel terrible if I let myself slow down and feel at all. He'd taken his divorce really hard, but the two scenarios weren't the same.

His ex-wife was the love of his life.

Em was...

For a moment, I considered undoing the icepacks and going back out for a jog, but unfortunately, the pinch in my joints were working into real pain.

Falling into my recliner, I kicked the footrest up and ignored the empty chair Em brought over from her house. I grabbed the remote control off the end table. My phone screen was still lit up, but it did not read Remi's name.

Adrenaline skyrocketed my pulse. My ears buzzed as I picked my phone up and read the screen. I didn't know what I expected, but it wasn't the no-nonsense message. It wasn't the complete void of the woman I'd fallen in love with.

***I'll grab my stuff while you're at work tomorrow. I'll leave your key and garage door opener on the table.***

It was all the confirmation I needed. My sliver of hope died.

She would grab the last of her things, leaving all signs of me behind when she left, and it'd be done.

It was probably for the best.

***K***, I responded.

Everything would go back to normal. It wasn't a bad life, but now I knew what life looked like with Em in it. It was like knowing the warmth of the sun, then living forever in overcast.

Fighting back the urge to tell her I was sorry, I set my phone back on the table.

Some things were better left never done. But my body felt like garbage, and my mind was trapped in a vice grip. I wanted my heart to be empty, but at that moment, it was full of grief and ache and need.

Indie's claws clicked on the floors as she took a few steps toward me. She laid her head on my thigh and whined. I reached my hand down to stroke the soft hair atop his head. "It's okay, sweetie, I'm okay." The words were barely a whisper in my empty home.

In her absence, I'd examined the night of the dinner and what I'd seen between her and Sam. With space and objectivity, it was clear I'd been insecure and jealous. It was humiliating to admit, even to myself. The realization didn't change anything, though. Because when it came down to it, I'd felt insignificant to her, and she'd cut me out like any other guy she'd dated.

My phone buzzed with an incoming call. I half-hoped it was Em, but this time, it was Remi. Pressing it to my ear, I answered, "Hello."

"Hey, man," he greeted in his gruff voice. "How you doin'?"

"I'm okay." It was mostly true. Now that my friend was on the phone, I had the distraction I needed.

"Yeah?"

A sarcastic smile lifted my lips. "Yeah. How are you?"

"I'm alright. I'm surprised you're not out running."

"I fell at work and my hip is all fucked."

"Oh, shit. You're becoming an old man like the rest of us."

I rolled my eyes. "Sure. I mean, you make it look so appealing with your bifocals and all."

He laughed. "Come on, I told you that in confidence, not so you can give me shit."

"They just sound really cool."

"Well, maybe someday you'll grow up to be a grown man with bifocals, too."

"Here's hoping." I looked at the clock on the microwave and tried to do the time zone math between here and Arizona. "You just get out of work?"

"Yup."

"How was it?"

"I got scratched to hell by a cat."

"I do not miss working with cats."

Then, in unison, we quoted a line from one of our vet school textbooks, "Never underestimate a cat."

I snorted. "You wanna watch something with me?"

"Sure. I heard about a really cool documentary about rodents and insects."

We stayed on the phone and watched the show. He threw in observations, while I grunted in agreement until it was time for me to force myself into my empty bed.

When my alarm went off the next morning, it was clear I'd made a terrible miscalculation the day before. My body was stiff in a very bad way. In a there-will-be-no-running-for-days kind of way. I opened the garage door to roll my bike out after getting Bandit in his weighted vest, but the fresh snow covering the ground made it clear that biking wasn't an option, either.

"Fuck." I looked down at him. "We're gonna have to walk, buddy."

It was bad for both of us, especially since walking left too much room for thinking.

# Chapter 22

## Emmeline

**K**. A single letter response. That one little letter shoved me right over the edge—an edge I've been teetering on for days. In my grieving process, I was somewhere between depression and pain. I couldn't stop replaying our argument over and over, wondering when I had just given up, and if he could forgive me for leaving. Wondering if I said I was sorry and that I'd fight for us in the future, would he take me back? But thanks to that single letter, I was violently shoved into acceptance.

It had been forty-eight hours since that heartbreaking **K**, and my acceptance had grown a sharp edge of anger. I hadn't found my way out of it yet.

I'd grabbed the last of my things. I even wrangled Tom into helping me, and together, we loaded up my chair.

The rage sifted away as I said goodbye to the dogs. Each of them with their unique reactions to me, from Venice's excited yips and Indie's apprehensive side-eye. Each one grated on my heart equally. I smiled and held the tears at bay as I said goodbye to them. But Maui's whimper as I scratched his little head tore my brittle heart in two.

By the time Tom and I got into my car, my throat hurt from holding back sobs.

The dogs didn't trust easily and leaving felt like a violation of the trust they'd given me.

When my tears grew too thick, I pulled into a grocery store parking lot and cried until my head and shoulders hurt. I should have trusted myself. I knew it would end like this... maybe not exactly this—I never envisioned myself sobbing outside of a Meijer—but I always knew we didn't stand a chance.

Tom offered to drive, and I nodded my response.

He held my hand as he drove. "Those dogs were emotional terrorists back there."

My laugh came out all blubbery. "Yeah. Like, I'm gonna be fine, ya know. Break-ups suck, but they happen. But those dogs—" The last sentence fell apart in a strangled squeak.

"What happened?"

I'd told my family that I was moving back home, but I hadn't given them any other context.

After a few deep breaths, I said, "He got jealous, and we decided it was best if we stopped."

"So, it's mutual?"

"Kinda. We didn't really talk about it."

"But this is what you want?"

I shrugged and shook my head. "I don't know."

I still didn't have an answer a day later.

I straightened and squared my shoulders. The blinds to my office were open, so I wouldn't shed any tears at work. Somehow, no one had noticed me and Owen fighting in the restaurant parking lot. There'd be less weathering of sympathy from my coworkers if I just kept a low profile, and this would blow over faster. Everything could go back to normal.

That's what I really needed. Some normal.

And a change in my clientele roster.

"Sam." I spun in my office chair. "You want Micheals' Builders?"

He looked up from his phone where he tapped out a message. "That's a huge client."

"I know. I don't want him. I deal with enough misogyny throughout the day, and I don't want to work with someone who equates my ability to do my job with my ability to be a wife."

"Can we just do that? Switch clients?"

"I don't know. It's not unheard of for relationships to go sour and get moved around. If you want him, I'll suggest you."

He looked through the window, and I could practically see the dollars and cents calculating like a mental spreadsheet. "I don't wanna work with that asshole," he said, shaking his head.

The small tug of a smile on my lips felt strange. "Thanks, man." The extra validation that I was making the right choice wasn't necessary, but it was appreciated.

I turned back around and emailed my dad and my sales manager, Lewis.

***

Stepping into my house used to feel like coming home, but I hadn't been able to find that feeling in the past week. It felt stale, like the house had forgotten how to be a home.

No dogs barked in welcome.

No one else to say hello to.

Just the emptiness of an empty building.

Maybe I should get a dog. But then I'd want to adopt from the shelter Owen worked at because, despite everything between him and me, the shelter was really wonderful. Just the idea of accidentally running into him did terrible things to my insides.

"No more big life decisions," I told myself. Dumping my bread-and-butter client today was probably enough for a while. I had savings, and I'd been building my other clients. It'd be a lean couple of months, but at least I wasn't going to lose my house.

How were the dogs doing? I hoped they weren't still sad, because that'd make the pain in my chest unbearable—rather than just nearly.

My phone buzzed on the counter where I'd thrown it next to my purse. The picture of Mom and me filled the screen. I took a moment to evaluate if I had the energy to answer it. Dad had probably told her about the email, and I knew she would want to talk reason into me.

It'd be better to rip off the band-aid than put off this conversation. "Hey, Mom."

"Hey, Em, how are you doing?" The gentleness in her voice made my throat knot.

*Ugh. So many emotions.*

"Fine. Did Dad tell you about the email?"

"What email?"

"Oh, I figured that's why you were calling."

"I was calling... 'cause you're sad, baby."

My throat squeezed. "Thanks, Mom."

I took deep breaths in the silence that followed. When I thought I might not sound like I was on the edge of tears, I said, "I'm giving up Micheals' Builders."

She gasped. "Why? That's... that's most of your roster, isn't it?"

"Yeah." Suddenly the lie I'd constructed was dust in my mouth. She had been supportive through every twist and turn, and she was still right there for me to lean on. I was sad, but not for the reasons she thought. I wouldn't tell her how I knew Michaels wouldn't work with me now that I was "getting a divorce." She should never have had to earn my honesty; she deserved it the whole time.

"Mom..." She couldn't see how my shoulders sunk under the pressure of the truth, or how my face burned red with shame. "I've been lying to you."

"What do you mean?" she asked after a pause.

"I was never married."

"What does that mean?"

"It was a lie. I lied to you."

"Why would you lie about that?" Her voice had dropped in warning, but she was still giving me an opportunity to explain myself.

The only way I could get the words out without them being drowned in emotion was to speak in a robotic monotone. "Micheals told me he wouldn't work with me because I was single, so I told him I was married... that I'd eloped. Owen had told Dutch he was married so Dutch would stop pushing him to date Laurie. New Year's Eve... it just... We doubled down. I'm so sorry, Mom."

I'd heard a loud silence before, but it had never been this deafening. It roared like the calm in the eye of the hurricane. Or that moment just before a car accident, where there's perfect clarity and no way to avoid the impact.

"I. Cannot. Believe. You." I hadn't heard that tone in so long, I felt like a child. "Jesus *Christ*, young lady. This is... I don't know if I've ever heard a crazier story."

"I know," I whispered.

"But you obviously love each other."

"No. Well... yeah—" My throat closed entirely around the last word.

She sniffed. "But you're not actually married."

"Correct."

"But you are in love."

"I don't know… It's complicated." I sank to the floor, my body too heavy to hold up anymore.

"Oh, Emmeline, you're… so *wrong* sometimes."

"What?"

"Of course, it's complicated. You've been pretending to be *married*. But what I am asking is, do you love him?"

"Yes," I choked out.

"Was being with him bad?"

"No."

"You expect things to be easy, but they're not."

"It's not that simple."

"It is."

"No—"

"You know what, fine," she cut me off. "You're the authority. I'm not arguing with you. God*damnit*, I am so mad at you." I jerked the phone away from my ear as her voice rose. When she spoke again, it was quieter. "Emmeline Patricia McCarthy, I'm so disappointed."

"Can you go back to being mad at me, because that's worse?"

There was a knock at the door.

"That will be the take-out I ordered for you," she exhaled. "I figured you weren't eating."

"Ugh. Mom, I really am so sorry."

"I know. Young lady, you know when you were little, and I told you there was nothing you could do that would make me love you less?"

"Mm-hmm," I forced out, anticipating what she was going to say next.

"That's still true. Eat your food. I already tipped them. Be kind to yourself and get some sleep."

"I love you," I spoke so quietly I didn't know if she could hear me.

"I love you, too. I'll talk to you tomorrow."

Pushing up from the floor, I went to the front door. My mom's love followed me like a shadow weaved with Owen's apathy, like water and oil, incapable of mixing.

I did eat the food—she ordered my favorite dish from my favorite Middle Eastern restaurant—and I did get some sleep. And I did try to be kind to myself.

***

"Let me be sure I understand this correctly," Dad said, his hands clasped on the conference tabletop. "Just before Christmas you approached Spencer Micheals with Micheals' Builders to establish a working relationship with him."

"Yes, and it wasn't my first attempt." I was having a hard time meeting his eyes. There was no way Mom didn't tell him about our phone call last night; he just hadn't brought it up yet. But then, if he wanted to talk about that, he wouldn't in a work meeting with Lewis.

"At that meeting, Micheals told you he wouldn't work with you because you were a single woman, for religious reasons."

My stomach lurched. "Yes."

"And now that you are going through a divorce, you feel that the same issue will arise?"

I noticed the slight pause just before the word *divorce*, but no one else would notice it. "Yes."

"Why didn't you come to us sooner?" Lewis asked.

*Because I was hoping to never get caught in my lie*, I admitted silently.

"I didn't like his implications... that I was indecent just because I was unmarried—and I told him something I wasn't planning on telling anyone yet. It was all so much more personal than I was prepared for... I was embarrassed."

Dad kneaded his forehead. He dragged in a deep breath and let his hands fall back to the tabletop.

Lewis turned the chair to face him. "What do you want to do?"

Without looking directly at Dad, I watched his mouth open, then close. He watched me for a moment. The clock above the door clicked away each passing second.

"I shouldn't make this call, I'm too biased. What do you want, Em?" he asked.

"I want him given to someone else—"

"That's the least that will happen." He leaned toward me and dropped his head in a silent will for me to meet his eyes. There was no use putting it off; he wouldn't speak until I did, and no one was more comfortable with silence than my dad.

I straightened my shoulders and met his gaze.

"What do you *want* to happen? What is the *best-case* scenario for *you*?" As usual, his words were intentional.

I sat up even straighter and squared my shoulders. What I was about to say would be unreasonable, but it was what he asked for. "I want him to take his business elsewhere. And I want him to know it's because he's a misogynist hiding behind his religion. If he can't work with women, then he should hire a manager to do it for him."

"That would be expensive," Lewis pointed out.

"He came for my livelihood when he wasn't willing to work with me. We shouldn't accommodate his bigotry. I would honor his current rentals because there are other businesses that would be affected negatively, but I don't want him to rent with us anymore."

Dad nodded. "That's more gracious than I would like, but it's good."

Lewis held his hands out. "Let's keep our heads. Micheals is a huge account."

"We won't go under because of one account," Dad reasoned.

"But we might lose other accounts because of this," Lewis pointed out.

"The good-ol' boys sticking together?" My fingers drummed on my knee.

"Let 'em." Dad clenched his fist on the tabletop. "Like I said, I'm probably too invested in the outcome."

"I need to think about this," Lewis said.

"It's okay if we keep him as a client. I know how this works." My words sounded deflated and empty.

"What do you mean 'how this works'?"

"We're a business; making money is our number one agenda."

His chest sunk in a sigh. "Thank you for understanding."

I nodded, but it turned into my head shaking. "You know, I'm sorry, I don't understand. Micheals decided his ethics were valuable enough *not* to work with me. Why do his ethics get more value than mine?"

Lewis and I jumped at the harsh pound of Dad's fist hitting the table.

"Ethics," he repeated, staring down at his fingers now splayed. "I'll be in my office."

Lewis and I remained in the room, but Dad's absence stayed present. Lewis promised to consider everything and have an answer for me by the end of the following workday.

Out of the conference room, my shoes clicked on the polished concrete floors of the hallway. I found my dad in his office where he said he'd be. It was positioned between the shop and the showroom, with a window facing both, as well as a window to the outside with a view of the yard, where booms, scissor-lifts, and other large equipment sat in wait.

His door was open, and I knocked on the frame.

He nodded toward the seat across from his desk. I didn't need him to tell me to close the door behind me—it was obvious our conversation was not meant for public consumption.

When I was seated, he began, "Your mom told me…"

My shoulders lifted toward my ears as my heart tightened in my chest. If I could have sunk into my chair, I would have. "I figured."

"Its… unbelievable to say the least."

"I know."

"Who all knows?"

"Mal, Tom, and Laurie."

He snorted, but there wasn't any humor in it. "I guess I'm glad they have your back, even when you don't make any sense."

I bit my lip.

"Why are you still wearing the ring?" He gestured to my left hand.

I ran my thumb over its smooth gold. "I can't get it off."

"Huh?"

"It's too small for my finger."

Stupid tears welled in my eyes. He turned in his seat and dropped the blinds to the shop before standing and doing the same for the window to the office.

Returning to his seat, he leaned back. "Why?"

It was a fair question—one I'd been asking myself for weeks now. I wiped a tear from beneath my eye and shrugged.

"Your mom says you're in love with that asshole."

"He's not an asshole, Dad."

"He sat at my table and lied to me."

"*I* sat at your table and lied to you."

"Do you lie to us often?"

"No."

"God, I hope not."

"I am sorry, Dad."

"I know." He sighed. "So, you love him?"

I took two deep breaths, hoping my voice would come out normal, but it was a whisper squeezed tight in my throat. Fat tears I couldn't stop soaked into the fabric of my pants. "Yes. I miss him so much."

"Goddamn it." I'd never heard his voice so harsh and rumbling in my life.

"I don't know how to make it up to you or Mom." I wiped my wet cheeks with the back of my hand.

"It's pretty shitty, and now I don't know what to think."

"I'm sorry," I said again, not knowing what else to say.

"I know."

We stared out the window at the equipment.

"Spencer Micheals is an ass," Dad said after a few minutes.

I snorted. "Yeah."

He shook his head. "I told Dutch I didn't want you dealing with him, but he was adamant that he'd be a good account for you. I should have... I knew he was a pain in the ass. I should have—"

"It's not your fault, Dad."

"Yeah..." He turned his attention to me, his eyes narrowed. An echo of my pain reflected in their blue depths.

"What?"

"I hate that guy."

"Micheals?"

"Owen."

"Don't. He's not a bad guy. He's actually really great. We just... made a mess of things."

"I don't care what kind of guy he is; I've watched my daughter walk around in pain for a week."

"I'll be okay, Dad." And it was true, even if it didn't feel like the truth at the moment. "Please don't hate him."

"Why?"

A sad smile grew on my face, and I shook my head. "Because I don't want anyone to hate him."

# CHAPTER 23

## OWEN

I heard Mr. Maynard before I saw him. My usual reaction would be to turn and escape in the other direction. That probably would have been the better choice, but instead, I rounded the corner, following the sound of his booming voice. I moved as quickly as my abused body would allow, though my four-day-old limp slowed me down. His voice carried over the dogs barking in their kennels, reverberating off the tile floor and concrete block walls. It was a big building, but I found him easily.

He was filling dog bowls. Mandi leaned against the counter, filling out charts.

Her smile faltered and froze when she saw me. "Owen, hi."

"Hey, Mandi," I returned, but I wasn't paying much attention to her. I was too busy noticing how Dutch's spine stiffened.

When he spoke again, it was the first time he'd ever reminded me of his brother, Simon—his volume dropped and the tone lowered. "I'll bring these to the dogs."

"I'll help," I offered.

"I'm sure you have other things to do."

I should have nodded and took the opportunity to disappear. It looked like Mandi wanted to disappear, I'd never seen anyone more focused on charting dog food.

The last conversation I had with Emmeline had ended with my texted, **K**.

My house didn't have any trace of her left.

I wanted to jog our normal trail on Saturday, but my body needed to recover from the fall and the strain I put it under last week. She wouldn't be there; I was pretty sure of that. Yet it was the only place I could look for her that wasn't creepy. I don't know what I would have done if I had seen her, and the thought caused me simultaneous pain and relief.

We couldn't go back to being friends; at least, I couldn't. The possibility of a relationship was burned and chard.

But I missed her.

I thought about her constantly.

Almost a week ago, I'd come home from work to find her key and garage door opener on my kitchen table. The chair she'd brought from her house was gone. The line of expensive looking bottles in the bathroom were gone, and the candles she'd bought that day at the mall were gone as well. I didn't need to check if her things were still hanging in the closet.

But I did anyway.

They weren't.

The cavern of my chest echoed with her absence.

I leaned against the doorframe, staring at the empty space until the dog's barks turned to whines. Then I layered on winter gear and took Bandit for a walk, full of angst that my pained body wouldn't let me outrun.

I was starving for her, and I would devour any crumbs I could find.

"I have time." I grabbed two bowls and just held them.

Dutch sighed. "You put them on the cart."

I found the gray plastic cart behind me. It squeaked as I rolled it the few feet to his workstation. Mandi took the opportunity to exit through the door I'd entered.

With another sigh, Mr. Maynard moved the bowls I'd obviously placed incorrectly. As he stacked the other dishes, I tried to help, but I ended up in the way more than anything else.

It was the first time I'd ever heard silence in the large man's vicinity. Every other time I'd been around him, I wondered how he could always have something to say—some joke or story to tell—and I wished he'd say something now.

When the cart was nearly full, I asked, "How's your family?"

The knuckles of the large hands holding the bowls went white. He straightened to his full height and width. I didn't know the man could expand like that.

"They're doing well, thank you for asking."

He took the handle of the cart and pushed it to the hall. He clearly didn't intend for me to follow, but I did.

"I'm glad to hear it."

Just before exiting the room, he stopped and turned. "How 'bout you ask what you really want to know?"

I shoved my hands into the pockets of my scrubs. I looked down at my shoes for just a moment before forcing myself to meet his eye. "How's Em?"

He nodded. He must have heard some of my desperation because his expression softened, but only slightly. "She's alright. You know Em... nothing keeps her down."

I didn't know if his words made it better or worse. I felt like I was missing something vital, like my leg or my arm. Something that I *could* live without, but I really didn't want to, and my life would be forever different without her in it.

I loved her, and I was glad she could move on.

But I loved her, and I wanted to be missed.

"Thanks." My quiet response was absorbed in the noises of dogs.

His big belly expanded with a deep breath. "Did you know about Micheals?"

I nodded.

The lines of his face deepened. His thoughts seemed to draw his gaze right through me. "I thought I was doing her a favor with that guy…" Then his gaze focused on to me. "I thought you would be good for her, too. Apparently, I've been very wrong."

That stung. Being lumped in with the client who had caused Emmeline so much grief, who had scared her into all of this, sat just about as well as an elephant on my chest. A muscle jumped in my jaw as I clenched my teeth, and any words in my defense were dry on my tongue.

I had seen what Micheals saw. I hadn't trusted Em more than my fears.

I hadn't been good to her.

"Dr. Kauahi, I really just wanna get this done." He swept a hand toward the cart in front of him. "And I'd really rather do it alone."

"Yeah, of course," I said to his back as he left me behind.

Instead of going directly to my office, I stopped by Journey. She barked excitedly when she saw me and dropped her face down with her tail wagging in the air.

Clipping a leash to her collar, I asked, "Will you hang out with me?"

She leaned her weight against my leg and smiled up with her tongue out.

"Thanks."

We hurried from one building to the other. In my office, she settled into the dog bed in the corner. I still felt disgusted with myself, but I appreciated her being there.

***

My mind was preoccupied with the conversation I'd had with Dutch, even after my walk with Bandit—mostly circling his comparison of me to the prick client, and the fact that I didn't have a defense. I'd been a jealous asshole, and I'd let it all end. I let her go; I hadn't fought for her, for us. I told myself it was for the best, but the longer I soaked in my thoughts, the more they became doubts.

Looking at the clock on my microwave, I decided Remi was probably driving home from his vet clinic.

He answered on the third ring. "Hey."

"Hey."

"What's up?"

I swallowed. "Have I fucked up completely?"

He sighed, not needing context. "I don't know, man. What do you think?"

I lowered into my recliner and rested a forearm on my thigh. "I don't know... maybe. We just gave up. We both just did what we normally do; I was a dickhead, and she wrote me off. But it's probably..." I had to swallow the knot in my throat before I continued, "Um, it's probably better it happened now and not in a couple of months or years or what-the-fuck-ever."

I withered, thinking of all the moments that could have been.

Remi's turn signal clicked over the speaker. "Why was it inevitable?"

Running a hand down my face, I leaned back in the chair. I spoke in a strangled whisper. "I don't know how to be different. I don't know how to trust."

"That shit with Natalie was fucked up."

The validation his words provided was something I hadn't known I needed. A third party who'd been there to see the manipulation. Sometimes I was so wrapped up in my head that I wondered what the events looked like from other people's eyes. If I'd made them into something they weren't.

"You never knew where you were at with her," Remi went on. "You remember that time we got drinks after taking our midterms, and she was pissed at you the whole night?"

I grunted an affirmation.

"Then she yelled at you to stop asking why she was mad."

"Then she got pissed at me for not caring that she was upset. And she talked shit about me all night." Regardless of the years that had passed since then, I recalled wishing I could go home without it being noticed. I wished I could shift everyone's attention anywhere but at me.

"It was shit like that all the time."

"Yeah..."

"It was fucked up. It's okay that you don't know what to believe."

Even though he couldn't see the tears welling in my eyes, I looked at the ceiling and tried to force them back. "I don't want to be alone. I want Em."

"Have you considered therapy?"

Just the thought of it made my anxiety spike. Talking openly with a stranger sounded like sick torture. I couldn't even find words to explain myself to the woman I loved, how could I be effective in therapy?

He didn't wait for me to answer. "I wish I'd looked for help when Alicia and I got together, before it all went shitty. I didn't fix my shit when I had the chance to save my marriage. I didn't do everything I could. I regret that... all the time."

He'd never talked like this with me before. I knew he'd been seeing a therapist for a while, but he never talked about it. Since their split, he hardly ever mentioned Alicia's name.

"I'm sorry, man," I said, unsure of what else to say.

"Have you tried talking to Em?"

"No, it's best I just leave her alone."

"Why's that?"

Maui let out a warning growl at Venice when she got too close.

"She's moving on. It'd be selfish to drag her back down," I said.

"Of course she's moving on, but she might change her mind if you told her how you feel."

"It doesn't matter. I already fucked up."

"What if she would rather forgive you? Isn't it selfish not to let her?"

"Why should she forgive me?"

"That's for her to decide. Look, I didn't try everything; I didn't say everything. There was nothing to lose, but I still held back. I lost my wife because of it."

"Em wasn't actually my wife."

"Doesn't mean you won't regret it."

I drew in a deep breath through my nose.

"You don't have to, but speaking from my end of things, I wish I had."

***

My finger hovered over Emmeline's contact the next day; all I had to do was tap the screen and through the wonders of technology, her phone would ring. Maybe she'd answer, maybe she wouldn't. I'd get to hear her voice either way, even her voicemail message would be welcomed.

My finger hovered.

"Fuck." I set my head on my desk. My lunch of soup and salad from a restaurant in town smelled delicious on the other side of my keyboard. I was too ridden with anxiety to eat it, even though I knew it was getting cold.

I sat up straight when I heard a conversation outside my closed door. It wasn't loud, but it carried against the hard surfaces of the hallway.

I was struck by the lightning bolt of dumb fucking luck.

Standing, my chair rolled to the other side of my office. It banged against a filing cabinet, but I was already through the doorway and into the hallway.

"Excuse me," I called.

# CHAPTER 24

## EMMELINE

"**A**re you gonna answer it?" Laurie asked.

My phone buzzed on the faux-wood tabletop in the breakroom. The picture of Owen that I hadn't had the heart to delete smirked on the screen.

Inside of me was a tumultuous turning of adrenaline and excitement. He was on the other side of that tiny device. All I had to do was answer it and I could hear him. I could talk to him. Missing him was so deeply nested in my marrow—like a wild vine growing up the side of a building—fingers drilled into nooks and crannies until there was no knowing if the structure would stand if the vine was removed.

Tears pricked my eye at the sight of his stupid lovely face forever trapped by the shutter of my camera.

I didn't know what he had to say. I was too scared to find out.

Laurie tilted her head for me to meet her eyes. "Do you want me to answer it?"

Pinching my lips together, I shook my head.

The circumstances that brought Laurie home were unfortunate. Her position at her advertising firm had been eliminated, so she had to sublet her place while she decided what to do next, while saving money living with her parents. I offered for her to stay at my house, but she refused until she had a job and could afford to pay rent. No amount of arguing had changed her mind, so instead, I helped with her job search.

We watched the phone buzz until it didn't anymore.

I wiped away a single tear that slipped past my control.

One more vibration announced his voicemail, and then silence.

"Do you want me to listen to it for you?" she offered.

I shook my head, still not trusting my voice. After another breath, I said, "I'll listen to it when I get home."

Her eyes went wide. "You can wait that long?"

"It's better than trying to listen to it here."

"Is it?"

"I don't know why he called. The last thing he said to me was—"

"*K* in a text message," she interrupted. "And we agree that is the lowest of low. But that's why I would listen to it *for* you."

A lot had happened since that final text. Micheals was invited to never rent from us again. There were a few accounts that took their business elsewhere, but not as many as I had thought. Turned out, Spencer Micheals was not well-liked.

The best part, especially with such a large hole in my roster and a broken heart, was that I had loads of time to hustle and build connections with my other clients. I wouldn't pull great numbers this month, but I was going to be okay.

"Then what?"

"If it's shitty, I delete it, and you can continue to not have any contact with him. But if it's not, then you know you don't have a shitty voicemail to listen to when you get home."

Both of our eyes drifted to the black box causing so much trouble.

I shoved it in her direction. "Okay."

I stood and left the room; I couldn't watch her face as she heard what he had to say. My expression was placid, and all the roiling ups and downs of my feelings were completely disguised as I walked across the showroom to my office. Sam jerked his head to greet me as he typed out an email. We both startled as Laurie slammed into our office and shut the door behind her.

"It's the white whale!" she hissed.

"What—"

"Shh!" She held her hands out, her fingers splayed.

Sam raised a questioning eyebrow at me.

I shrugged. "What the fuck are you talking about?"

She punched my passcode into my phone. "It's the white whale. Owen got you a meeting."

The speaker pressed against my ear was silent for half a second, and then he was talking. There was a tone in his voice that calmed the scattered vibrations inside me. It set me to hum at the right frequency.

"Hey Em..." he began.

My eyes closed.

"I..." He sighed, then groaned. "Look, MacIntosh is in town, and he's agreed to a meeting. He's only available tonight. I told him who you are and where you work and... I'm sorry, I wish I had more warning for you... and... I hope this doesn't hurt you, but will you pretend to be my wife one more time? Anyway... um, let me know. Bye, Em."

Pretend to be his wife again? When the sound of his voice made all my pieces realign and the silence that followed sent them scattering.

I shook my head. "I can't do it."

I felt the energy rush out of Laurie. "Right. Of course. I was just possessed by the energy of my father and went full extra. Of course, you can't. I should have realized—"

"Can't what?" Sam asked. He must have been very curious because he normally could only communicate in grunts when Laurie was around.

"Owen set up a meeting with Bill MacIntosh for tonight, but she'd have to pretend they're still together," Laurie explained.

Sam sucked in a sharp breath.

I opened my eyes. "Can I do that?"

Her shoulders lifted and her mouth hung open as if waiting for words to come out. "Can you?"

"Should I?"

She shrugged again, her palms up. "Maybe it's because… my career has gone to garbage, but yes. Yes, you should. It took my dad *thirty years* to get in the same room with that guy. You can do this, Em. And if you don't, the opportunity will never come again."

I tapped the wedding band I still hadn't taken off against my phone. Shaking my head, I opened my text app and clicked on Owen's name. That haunting *K* was at the bottom of the screen until I sent:

**When and where?**

***

The irony of meeting Owen at The Mills Center where the New Year's Eve party had been held did not escape me. We agreed to meet at the elevators outside The Stadium banquet hall before walking to the restaurant just outside the lobby of the hotel. I was nervous at the idea that he'd be there waiting for me, and I was nervous at the idea that I'd have to stand there waiting for him. I was nervous that we'd hug, and I was nervous that we wouldn't.

What was I even doing here?

Yes, I wanted this client, but not *this* badly.

In truth, I wanted to see Owen.

A clean break had never hurt like this. Cutting myself off from a relationship meant discomfort that ebbed away. Cutting myself off from Owen had had the exact opposite effect.

"Hey." His voice behind me made me stop short and my stomach drop like I was at the top of a roller coaster.

I turned and laid eyes on him, and the nerves stayed, but they were overwhelmed by relief. He was here. Our oxygen was the same, richer somehow because of his proximity.

I'd just... left.

The world was brighter around him, and I'd left it.

I left him.

We just gave up.

His chest sank with a quick exhale.

We stood three feet apart. I couldn't stop staring at him, at the sharp lines of his lips and the high angle of his cheekbones. He wore a forest-green sweater and dark jeans. The green in his eyes stood out against their golden browns. How had I ever described his eyes as hazel when they were a kaleidoscope of colors and shapes? A single word could never express such complexity.

He pushed his fists into his pockets and shrugged.

"Hi." I forced my voice to sound casual.

A muscle jumped in his jaw.

"How are you?" I asked as he said, "Thanks for coming."

"Sure," I said as he answered, "I'm okay, you?"

I chuckled and he smirked.

I pulled my hair over my shoulder. "Yeah, I'm alright. Not feeling awkward at all."

That won me a full smile.

"Good, that makes two of us."

"Just two very not awkward adults."

"That sounds like us." His Adam's apple bounced as he swallowed. He took half a step toward me, lowering his voice to a whisper. "How have you been?"

Keeping an air of nonchalance was difficult. "Good. Busy. You?"

He grunted, and I didn't know what to make of it.

"Uh, we should probably get in there."

"Sure."

The idea of him touching me for any other reason than he wanted to made my insides feel like they were in a meat grinder, but I held my hand out to him, anyway.

It stayed there, suspended between us. He stared at it, and I almost drew it back, but then his fingers curled between mine. Our palms pressed together, and the meat grinder went up in speed.

When I looked up from our joined hands, I found him watching me. There was heat and something else in his eyes—a reflection of the longing seated deep inside of me.

"It'll look better if we're holding hands, right?" I whispered.

"Do you want to hold my hand?"

"It's fine."

He opened his mouth, then shook his head. Taking a deep breath, he squared his shoulders. "Are you ready to be charming?"

"Are you saying I'm not always charming?"

"I would never say something so foolish."

I raised an eyebrow. "You told people you were married."

"Still less foolish than implying that you aren't *always* charming."

I smiled down at our shoes. "I'm ready."

The restaurant was busy, but quiet. The lighting was just a touch above dim. We were shown to a table where an average-looking man in his late sixties sat. Mr. MacIntosh was excessively normal—average height, nondescript face, and nice manners. I expected the man that everyone referred to as the white whale to be more like Dutch.

We talked shop through dinner. Owen watched me as much as was polite, with an adoring curve to his lips that gave me heart palpitations.

My hand resented the fork it held instead of his hand.

When dinner ended, MacIntosh promised to look over our rates.

Owen held my hand again.

The three of us walked across the skywalk to the parking garage as we exchanged polite conversation. I told the story of my dad and uncle starting the business, being sure to pepper in anecdotal humor.

The warmth of early spring had left with the setting sun and a wintry wind gusted through the concrete structure.

"I'll send your rates to our business manager, who's the real decider here." MacIntosh shook my hand.

"Understood. I appreciate you taking the time to chat with me."

"Dr. Kauahi spoke so highly of you. I can see why he's so biased."

"Thank you again," Owen said.

We walked hand in hand in the opposite direction of MacIntosh. After a few steps, Owen asked, "Where are you parked?"

"Top level. You don't have to walk me."

Instead of answering, he kept at my side to the stairs. As a group of excited, early twenty-somethings climbed down, we had to walk single file with me behind him. There was a hitch in his step on his right leg.

"Are you limping?"

"Uh, yeah, it's getting better now, though." He waited for me to join at his side before continuing to my car. It was easy to spot with most of the spots on this level empty. The sky over our heads was inky blue, a few stubborn stars burned bright enough to be seen through the light pollution.

"What happened?"

"Slipped at work, and then overdid the running."

Rocks scraped on the concrete under our shoes as we closed the distance to my car. Leaning my hip against it, I faced him. A lock of my hair blew across my face.

He moved to brush it back, but hesitated inches from touching me.

We were trapped in amber, questions rich in both of our eyes. We were in unknown territory, and I didn't know what feelings I could trust—and I had a lot of feelings. They ricocheted in my chest, an echoing chamber of love and fear.

"Why did you set this up, Owen?" I clutched the collar of my coat closed under my chin.

He cupped the back of his neck. In the sleeve of his sweater, his bicep flexed against the fabric. "I wanted to talk to you, but I didn't know if you wanted to talk to me."

My eyebrows pinched together.

"That makes it sound like manipulation. Fuck, maybe it was. Fuck." His hands dug deep into his jeans pockets, and he shrugged. "You asked for this meeting, and I wanted to give it to you."

"Thank you for the meeting."

He nodded. "You're welcome."

I scraped the pointed toe of my flats against the concrete. "What did you want to say?"

"I'm sorry. I'm so fucking sorry."

"Me, too," I breathed. "I shouldn't have just left. I'm so sorry."

"I didn't stop you."

"You aren't responsible for my actions."

"I miss you." He came closer. His hand hovered near my hip, as if he wanted to touch me but wouldn't.

The wind gusted again, carrying the scent of wintergreen and the indescribable scent of Owen. I wanted to sink into it, press my face to his neck, and just breathe.

He cupped my hip and squeezed, and I felt the contact everywhere.

I gave in and rested my head on his shoulder, the wool of his sweater soft against my cheek.

"Em." His arms wrapped around my back. His stomach pressed to mine. I felt his heart beat against my chest. There wasn't room for the defenses I'd built between us.

They crumbled, and it terrified me.

"I miss you, too." My lips brushed against his neck.

"Can we try again?"

I squeezed my eyes shut against the sting of tears. "I want to... But how will it be different? I know I can't just run away, I know I have to fix that. But it has to be different, you know?"

"I've been thinking about this." He leaned back to look at me. "We could go back a few steps, you know? I'd take you out on a real first date. Pick you up at your place, then drop you off at the end of the night. We'd slow down. What do you think? Can I take you out sometime?"

"I want to say yes."

"Okay, let's go another step back. Can I call you sometime?"

I bit my lower lip as my mouth spread into a smile and nodded.

Dimples pressed into his cheeks. He rested his forehead against mine. "I want to kiss you so badly."

Like the stubborn stars, hope burned in my chest. "Then do it."

He shook his head. "I can wait."

"But what if I can't?"

His eyes dropped to my mouth, his resistance waned before it snapped back into place. "There's nothing slow about our kisses, Em."

I hated it, but he had a point.

"Okay, I'll wait."

He stepped back. "I'll call you."

"Okay, goodnight, Owen."

"Goodnight."

He waited to walk toward the stairs until I was buckled in my car and the engine was running. I waited until I couldn't see his dark hair as he descended to the lower level before setting the gear shifter into drive. A second later, my phone buzzed.

I grinned so hard it hurt as I answered, "This is you going slow?"

"You still have your clothes on. I've exercised as much restraint as I have available. How was your day?"

"It turned out pretty great, actually."

"Yeah? Mine, too."

# CHAPTER 25

## EMMELINE

For our first date, Owen had taken me to dinner and a movie. Even though I caught him looking at me in my jeans and crop top sweater like he could see through them, all he did that night was walk me to my door and kiss me goodnight. It was only a soft brush of his lips on mine, and when he pulled away, the need for more was clear in his eyes.

We hiked a nearby county trail for our second date. The ground was soggy from freshly melted snow, and steam rose off the quarry. At the back of the trail, we climbed a steep incline. Using our hands, we gripped protruding roots. By the time we were at the top of the hill, my hands were covered in dark mud. I glanced between my dirty hands and my cute hiking gear, disappointed that I didn't have anything else to clean them on.

"Here." Owen wrapped his fingers around my wrists and wiped them down the front of his shirt, which did very little to conceal the hard surface of his chest and abs.

Cupping his pecs, I said, "Oh no, my hands are just filthy."

"Are they?" He lifted an eyebrow.

"So dirty."

His sliver of restraint broke, and he pushed me against a tree where we made out until my lips were numb and I'd dry-humped him to my orgasm.

"Fuck," he groaned. "You look like you were mauled by a bear."

My head was too foggy. All I could think about was his erection pressed against my hip.

"What?" I gasped, still trying to catch my breath.

"I might have lost my fucking mind."

Later, when I got to my aunt and uncle's to pick Laurie up, she threw a scarf at me before her parents could see me. "Put this on, you deviant! Going slow, huh?"

"What?"

She narrowed her eyes and shook her head.

I excused myself to the bathroom before we left for game night at Tom and Malcolm's. Under the scarf I'd tied round my neck was a bright red hickey and the scrape of teeth on my skin.

I invited Owen to dinner at my place for our third date.

Carl was outside spreading mulch when I opened the door and let Owen in. We waved, and I pulled Owen inside before Carl could start any small talk.

The door shut behind him, and he narrowed his focus on my face and body. His head tilted, taking in the way my skirt followed the curve of my hip, then up to the deep V of my sweater. His look alone scattered me. If he touched me in any way, I'd catch on fire. My breath grew short as my chest rose and fell.

He stalked slow steps toward me until my back was against my foyer wall.

Standing close enough that I could feel the heat coming off his body, he said, "Dinner smells good."

"Thank you."

"Can it wait?"

"Yes."

I flung myself around him, and my legs clung to his waist. His mouth was on mine, demanding and urgent. The hem of my skirt dug into my thighs until he pushed it up above my hips. His hands slipped under my panties to squeeze the fullness of my ass. I arched my back and moaned. He scraped his teeth down my neck, and I knotted my fingers in the silky strands of his hair.

I was desperate for him—not just for his touch or his skin against mine, but for *him*. For the moments when we were both laid completely bare, to be seen and loved for the parts that we kept hidden.

To be unguarded, but safe.

He pushed his hand between our bodies. I was delirious from the pressure; the sound of him unzipping his jeans made me aware of the small coverless window in the front door.

"Window," I gasped.

His hands went back to my ass, and he hoisted me up. The muscles of his shoulders and back flexed as he carried me further into my house, around a corner, and against my hallway wall.

"Condom?" He pulled his wallet out of his back pocket.

"No, please."

He pulled my sweater down. My jaw dropped as he pinched and stroked my nipple. His mouth replaced his hand, and a moan tore through me. His groan rumbled in my spine. With his finger, he hooked my panties out of the way.

His cock was at my entrance.

He moved the hand at the base of his shaft to press flat against the wall by my ear. My nipple popped from his swollen, wet lips. His eyes were yearning as he held my gaze.

My breath caught in my throat as he pushed inside me, burying himself to the hilt in one slow, smooth stroke.

"Fuck, Em," he said through quick breaths. "I'll be tender next time, but right now… I fucking can't. You feel so fucking good." He pulled out and pushed back into me with each sentence. He moved faster and faster until he set a punishing pace that I met stroke for stroke. Gripping the fabric of his shirt, he hit a place inside me that made my toes curl and stars dance behind my closed eyes.

It was urgent and hungry. I was consumed with his sharp breaths in my ear and the scent of his sweat beading on his forehead.

I fell apart within minutes, crying out and pulling his hair. Within seconds, he followed me, squeezing my thighs.

He let go of my legs. We stood pressed against the wall, catching our breath. Wrapped in each other's embrace, we shared the burden of balance. Eventually, he lifted his head from my shoulder. His kaleidoscope eyes met mine, and a dimple pressed into his cheek.

"Hi," he said.

Smiling, I pressed my forehead to his. "Hi."

I'd wisely decided to make a crockpot potato bacon soup and good thing, because after the hallway, we found our way to my bedroom.

"So, this is what it's like to have a sofa that doesn't belong to a St. Bernard?" He held a bowl of soup in one hand and his spoon in the other. Leaning into the corner between the armrest and the back cushion, his bare feet sat propped on my coffee table. His jeans were unbuttoned, and he wasn't wearing a shirt.

I nodded. My feet extended on the cushion between us, my bowl of soup on my lap. "But there's also no Ella here. How are the dogs doing?"

"Good. They'll be excited to see you."

I almost didn't ask because I'd been avoiding the question for the past couple of weeks. "Did they miss me?"

"They're okay. They'll be happy to see you," he said again.

"I have good news."

"What is it?"

"MacIntosh is going to give me a chance."

His eyebrows shot toward his hair. "Really?"

I nodded. "It's just one job site, but it's an opening."

"I knew it. That dinner—" He grinned broad and goofy. "I fucking knew it. You did so well. Congratulations."

I was certain my exposed chest and neck were bright pink with a pleased blush. "I also offered for McCarthy Rentals to host a dog adoption party. I can't imagine that'd hurt."

An impressed grin spread across his lips. "It was a good move."

"Thanks."

After cleaning up our bowls and getting the rest of the soup in the fridge, we went back to bed. I laid on my side and took in the slopes of his profile as he told me about the therapist he'd started speaking to.

"I've never done this before, so I don't have anything to compare him to, but I think it's a good fit. I'm not comfortable talking to him, but I'm not uncomfortable either. It's just kinda strange, you know?"

My cheek dragged against the soft fabric of my pillowcase as I nodded. "I can see why it would be strange. Are you getting anything out of it?"

"Well, I told you I'm going to therapy and I'm only a little anxious about what you might think of that. So yeah, I think it's helping."

"I think it's great." I slipped my hand down his wrist and entwined my fingers in his.

He sighed and rolled onto his side to face me. "Thanks."

It was too dark for me to see all the colors of his eyes, but I knew the kaleidoscope was there. I knew all the different shades of him and that there were depths still to discover. And I knew I had depths he hadn't seen yet, either. But I had a newfound trust in myself and him. We were tied together through a force of will, respect, and love.

"I'm so glad you're here," I whispered, my eyes drifting closed.

His voice sounded peaceful and sleepy. "I'm glad to be here."

# EPILOGUE

## OWEN

Emmeline claimed she merely mentioned the adoption party that she needed to coordinate on behalf of the shelter to Dutch. But once he knew about it, the event was out of her hands. He'd brought in multiple food trucks and dog trainers to help the potential adopters with basic obedience skills. He'd even hired a string quartet to play under the large white tent.

"Your uncle has a knack for parties," I said. Taking a bite of my fancy food truck grilled cheese, I looked around. "There's a ton of people here, but it's pretty calm. It's a good setting for the dogs."

"He's pretty great," she agreed.

We were both volunteering for the event, as were pretty much her entire family. Only Malcolm and Tom were off the hook, but they were expected to show up in support. Sam agreed to cover Em and me at the T-shirt table while we ate our food.

We sat side-by-side and I held her hand in my lap. Her skin was soft and warm as I drew circles with the pad of my thumb. People milled around us, unaware that my world was thrown off-kilter and set right again. She glanced over her shoulder and gave me a pleased smile.

It pushed the air from my lungs.

I wanted to close the distance between us and press my lips to hers, but we were at my work. Instead, I lifted our joined hands from my thigh and kissed the back of hers.

"I love you," I whispered.

"I love you, too." She tilted her head. "What are you thinking?"

It was a question I was getting more used to, and one her therapist had suggested she get more comfortable asking.

I shrugged. "Gratitude, I guess. It's a nice day... and I'm here with you."

Understanding and appreciation warmed her eyes. "Yeah, me too."

Her focus shifted over my shoulder. "Oh my god, Laurie, you look ridiculous with her. She could drag you and not even know you were there."

A few feet away, Laurie walked with Journey attached to a leash. I wasn't sure if Laurie made Journey look larger or if Journey made Laurie look smaller, but it was absolutely ridiculous.

Giving the leash a gentle tug, Laurie guided the Great Dane in our direction. She sat on a white plastic folding chair across from us.

"I know, but she's such a babe." She scratched under the dog's ear and cooed. "I can't believe no one has taken her home yet."

"People get intimidated by a big dog and medical issues." I pushed the last bite of my sandwich into my mouth and wiped my face with a napkin.

"You could adopt her." Em raised an eyebrow.

Rolling her eyes, Laurie shook her head. "I can't. I don't have a home."

"I'm your landlord, and I'm saying it's fine."

It'd only been a little over three months since Laurie had moved back, first with her parents, then as Emmeline's roommate after she was hired as an administrator at McCarthy Rentals—before Em officially moved in with me almost four weeks ago.

Laurie's voice was gentle as she said, "You know it's temporary. I'm outta here as fast as I can make it happen."

Emmeline's bottom lip stuck out in the most enticing way. I had to remind myself that we were at my work.

"Fine," she said.

"Sorry, bestie," Laurie went on in an imitation of her dad. "Have you met Sam? Have you met Sam yet? Good-lookin' fella, doncha think? He's a good-lookin' guy. Quite the catch."

"That sucks." I cringed, remembering how insistent her dad could be.

"It does," she agreed.

Swishing her ponytail, Emmeline leaned on the table. "Okay, but *have* you met Sam?"

Laurie rolled her eyes. "We work in the same building. We've met."

"Oh, then you *know* he's gainfully employed. Real nice guy."

"Don't."

"I'm just saying... maybe chat him up."

"He's *silent*. I'm not convinced the man can speak."

"He's just a little shy."

Leaning closer, Laurie lowered her voice to just above a whisper. "Look, I know what you're doing, and it's not a good look on you. Plus, I only have patience for my dad to be this annoying."

"You know, your dad's not always wrong; maybe you should give him a chance."

Em was unaffected by the glare her cousin bore into her. With forced politeness, Laurie asked me, "Will you keep an eye on Journey?"

I nodded and took the leash.

Standing, she marched in the direction of where Sam was selling T-shirts.

Under the table, I bumped Emmeline with my knee. "What was that about?"

She beckoned Journey to her, and the dog's tail wagged aggressively. "I can guarantee that Laurie is making it clear to Sam that she's leaving town as soon as possible, and there's no chance she'll start a relationship with anyone. Which means some of his anxiety will chill out and he can start being normal around her. It's... *unbearable* to watch."

"It's that bad?"

"Owen, it's *terrible*."

"Poor guy." To my astonishment, I did feel sympathy for him. Maybe it was feeling more secure with Em or the therapy I'd been going to, but I hoped he could find a way to cope.

"Who is this beauty?" Tom asked from behind me.

Journey's tail wagged even harder.

"Isn't she lovely?" Em stood to hug her brother and brother-in-law.

I joined her and shook their hands. "This is Journey. She's one of my favorite dogs."

Mal scratched her side. "I hardly have to bend to pet her."

The next couple of hours moved at an easy pace. Em shot me an excited expression every time Mal, Tom, and Journey were in sight. They stayed and helped clean up the folding tables and chairs, and they stopped by her kennel before they left.

I let down my professionalism for just a moment to pull Em's back against my chest.

She leaned her head back against my shoulder and gazed at the blue summer sky. "It's a good day."

Nuzzling my nose into her neck, I nodded. "It is."

Loved this? Check out my novella Truth or Daire

Serena Jackson falls hard when handsome stranger Daire O'Dowd swoops in as her skirt and the Windy City conspire against her. But as she's flying high, he turns out to be her new subordinate—and completely off-limits. Canceling their date is easier than ignoring her desire for him, which only grows more intense as the months tick by. When Serena discovers someone is embezzling from the PR firm they work at, it seems as if Daire might be the #1 suspect. Struggling not to fall head-over-heels in love with the handsome Irishman starring in all of her fantasies, Serena must determine whether he's innocent or guilty.

Daire has a secret—and it's concealed better than the lust he has for his boss. Keeping it hidden grows harder when an unfortunate booking error forces them to share a room... And a bed.

**_Can they resist temptation so delicious?_**

"Truth or Daire is a steamy, sizzling romp with delightful banter and a meet-cute for the ages! This is office romance done right, and I can't wait for more from Marty Vee! "

-Roxie Noir

https://www.amazon.com/dp/B0B1W3FYND

# ACKNOWLEDGEMENTS

I'm so happy to thank my friend and developmental editor Mika Rekai! She is a constant source of encouragement, and the way she shares her knowledge of storytelling has made me a better writer. Thanks, Mika!

Thank you, Silvia Curry, for your proficient copy edits, and proof-reading, and being awesome to work with!

And to Kate Prior, who did my cover and a lot of my promotional graphics, I've said it before and I'll say it again, you don't even know how good you are. However good you think you are, you're better.

To my sweet little Smut Coven, you're critiques and thoughts made this book better, and I've grown through your friendships too. You're all just, like, the cutest!

I want to thank my husband, kids, and mom, for being excited with me, and talking me through the challenges of writing this book.

The character Dutch is loosely based on my grandpa's cousin, Mason Eugene, but to me, he was Uncle Dutch. He was a larger-than-life character, who cheated at cards, was banned from playing carnival games at Cedar Point—because he always won—and told the most outlandish stories. He was an only child, but his mom claimed that was because he was everything wrapped up in one—the sweetheart, the troublemaker, and the goofball. I have never met anyone anything like Uncle Dutch and he is greatly missed.

Finally, a big "I don't know what I'd do without you" to my friend Danielle. Part of the inspiration for this book was Danielle's love, commitment, and anecdotes from working at an incredible dog shelter in our area. She's often one of the first people to read my books, as well as, to hear any news. She's amazing! My golden haired, sunflower of a bestie! Love you, Nell!

# Books



*Truth or Daire*

Serena Jackson falls hard when handsome stranger Daire O'Dowd swoops in as her skirt and the Windy City conspire against her. But as she's flying high, he turns out to be her new subordinate—and completely off-limits. Canceling their date is easier than ignoring her desire for him, which only grows more intense as the months tick by. When Serena discovers someone is embezzling from the PR firm they work at, it seems as if Daire might be the #1 suspect. Struggling not to fall head-over-heels in love with the handsome Irishman starring in all of her fantasies, Serena must determine whether he's innocent or guilty.

Daire has a secret—and it's concealed better than the lust he has for his boss. Keeping it hidden grows harder when an unfortunate booking error forces them to share a room... And a bed.

***Can they resist temptation so delicious?***

"Truth or Daire is a steamy, sizzling romp with delightful banter and a meet-cute for the ages! This is office romance done right, and I can't wait for more from Marty Vee!"  -Roxie Noir

*All Roads to Carter*

He's got her all turned around...

Ten years ago, Margo Reynolds and her high school crush, Carter James, didn't kiss. It didn't derail their friendship, but she didn't forget it either.

She returns to her hometown a failure, and yet he's hotter than ever. The boy who drove her crazy has become the man who drives her wild.

Can she open herself up to the possibilities Carter offers, when she feels hollowed out from abandoning her dream of acting? A dream that has taken so much from her and left her with no idea what path to take.

# MARTY VEE IN THE WILD

**M**arty Vee lives in Michigan with her wonderful husband, two wild kids, a tenderhearted dog, and two troublesome cats. She loves reading, and hiking, and generally being outside.

Vee is for Romance Readers Group

https://www.facebook.com/groups/1161878791021065
The Tiktok

https://www.tiktok.com/@martyveeauthur
Instagram

https://www.instagram.com/martyveeauthor/
Twitter

https://twitter.com/MartyVeeAuthor
Romance Writer's Therapy Podcast

https://romancewriterstherapy.buzzsprout.com/

www.ingramcontent.com/pod-product-compliance
Lightning Source LLC
Chambersburg PA
CBHW070504300726
48975CB00007B/2310